ADVENTURA HIGHWAY

ADVENTURA HIGHWAY

by
Lonya Avery

Everlasting Publishing
Yakima, Washington
USA

Adventura Highway

by
Lonya Avery

ISBN-13: 978-0-9983858-5-3

"Adventura Highway" is purely a work of fiction so any
resemblance to actual persons, places, and events depicted
therein is only coincidental and not to be taken seriously.

Lonya Avery

Second Edition
Everlasting Publishing
P.O. Box 1061
Yakima, WA 98907

ADVENTURA HIGHWAY

ADVENTURA HIGHWAY

Prologue

It was a windy cold afternoon in Fierro, New Mexico that early January. The thin sunlight that was piercing though the clouds and past the ochre-colored buttes touched on a man of sturdy, though short build. He was standing dazedly and shivering against a road sign which read Albuquerque 226 miles. His face was pale and his tawny eyes behind his aviator glasses looked glassy and almost lifeless. One might even have compared them to those of a doll or manikin.

Suddenly, a gust of bone-chilling wind blew a section of a newspaper past his feet. But the half-alive, half-frozen figure standing slumped against the road sign didn't notice it at all. Instead, he was thinking of the last place where he'd been warm – Hillcrest General Hospital at Silver City. Unfortunately, that was also where he had been coldly informed by the hospital staff that he could no longer stay there due to lack of money on his part. They had turned him out into the cold literally while he was still recovering from a severe head injury. It began to snow.

Just then, a car appeared out of the windy, deathly chill. It was a white 1935 Amilcar Pégase. Behind it was a hauler carrying two professional-looking motocross cycles. The driver was a thin-faced, blond fellow whose jacket was as white as the snow that was wafting along on the blustery wind. He pulled up right beside of the near-frozen man who had gamely put his thumb up in one last hope of a ride.

"Hi dude. Hop right in," the white-clad gentleman invited in a voice that was deep, comforting, and rich with a Nebraskan accent. When he saw that the hitch hiker was having trouble getting into his car, he left his front seat and helped him in.

"So, where you headed on such a cold, windy day?" asked the stranger in white as his passenger settled down into the warm comfort of the seat beside him.

"Anywheres," the man gasped, "as far from Silver City as I can get."

As they drove along, the thin driver asked a few more questions of the dazed, ill man beside him while the radio played "Ventura Highway", a hit song by the rock group America. He learned that his name was James Schönhausse and that he had barely recovered from a near-fatal motorcycle accident. When the pallid, spare driver learned that last detail, he drove all of the way to Las Cruces and checked James into the hospital there.

Before leaving him in the care of the medical staff, he had paid them enough money to ensure that James Schönhausse would receive the best care from them as long as he needed it. And he could more than afford to do so. He was multimillionaire celebrity motocross racer and daredevil stunt driver Adolf "Addy" Geisst, on his way to do a thrilling 190 mile leap in Las Cruces.

***

Chapter One

I was standing by the side of the road one wintry South Dakota morning in 2012 when a sturdy man with an impish grin drove near me in a bright red Ford Festiva. I was holding a sign that read "Will Work For Food". He stopped by me and made a sarcastic remark. In response, I flipped him the birdie. He laughed and then drove on.

A week later and I was standing by the shoulder of the freeway again. This time I had traded my sign for a small accordion and a little monkey. The same sturdy man pulled up beside me, only now his manner was more friendly than teasing.

"Will you come with me and live a life of hardship, pretty circus girl?" he asked me.

Not able to resist his expressive light-brown eyes, stocky physique, and invitation to an adventure, I replied in the eager affirmative.

"Sure, I'll come along for laughs, cute guy."

He gave me a wink and then helped me load myself and my performing pet into his little red car.

"Hi, I'm Bonnie Barry and this is Taffy," I said after my little monkey and I had settled down in the seat beside this fascinating driver. "And you're...?"

"James Schönhausse," he answered as he shook my hand in a way that was gentle and at the same time firm.

As we rode along, James asked me where I was headed. I told him Moose jaw, Saskatchewan. I in turn asked him what his destination was and he told me Dickinson, North Dakota where he had a job waiting for him at the city's newspaper office. I expressed a desire to ride with him to Dickinson and apply with the paper myself. He invited me to go for it, especially when I told him that I had written articles for *The Caribou Bugle*, a community newspaper circulating in the British Columbian town of Quesnel.

James and I stopped for lunch at a park just across the border between South and North Dakota. Staying in the warm vehicle, we enjoyed a meal that both of us had contributed to. He happened to have some pieces of chicken in a styrofoam food box, while I had a couple of apples in my handbag. Together, we, including Taffy, enjoyed a simple, but fulfilling breakfast. Fulfilling because the plainest meal, eaten in good company, can seem like a banquet.

James and I were indeed really enjoying each others company. As we both finished munching on our apples, he tenderly took me by the hand and told me that I was "pretty, very pretty." Honored by his kind words I squeezed his hand affectionately and told him that he had muscles to die for.

"Believe me, I've worked hard building 'em all my life," said James as he returned my hand-squeeze.

"You work with weights, cute guy?" I ventured to ask with growing interest.

"Yes and I've even won some trophies in weight-lifting competitions, circus sweetie."

"I can tell you do. You have a marvelous physique."

"Why thank you."

With our meal finished, we were back on Highway 94 again.
Soon we were passing by a landscape of bentonite buttes on which
snow was collecting, making their smooth tops and rugged fins
all the whiter. James and I started talking about these imposing
rock pillars, avid geologists that we both were. Then he looked
down and noticed the rock I was wearing. It was a smooth green
aventurine stone on a fine gold necklace.

"Sure is a beautiful piece of aventurine. It's a form of quartz
and its name stems from 'aventura,' which is Italian for 'by
chance'," James said as he leaned away from his steering wheel
and gave my pendant a closer look.

"Aventura! Sort of like my favorite song, 'Ventura Highway',"
I said beaming.

"One of the rock group America's greatest hits," said James
beaming back.

He and I then dropped the subject of rocks and launched into
a discussion about the truly made in the USA 70s rock band and
their many hit songs. On cue, James popped a CD into the car's
music player and soon the three of us were swept along by a
whole album of America's lively, smooth-rocking tunes.

With the music to speed us along, we rode past miles of flat,
snow-draped fields, small towns, and the occasional ghost town.
When we passed by the derelict burg of Curlew with its distin-
guishing iron arch, we met up with a hitch hiker who was a tall
blond fellow dressed all in white. James picked him up and gave
him a ride down to the nearest gas station which was a Texaco.
After we dropped him off there, he thanked us and gave James
two $100 bills. James wished him luck, gassed up, and soon

we had returned to the highway. As we rode away, we waved back at our erstwhile passenger who appeared to vanish into the shadows which were as dark and foreboding as the sheets of black ice that were starting to collect on the road under us.

Before long, we were on the outskirts of the town of McKenzie, a place just outside the sprawling city of Bismarck. By then it was very late and James decided it was time for all of us to bed down. With that in mind, he found a woodsy roadside pull over and parked the Festiva in it. Me and Taffy would sleep in the front seat part, while he would sleep in the back. The lingering warmth from the little car's heater would keep us all cozy along with eiderdown blankets and pillows.

"Good night, sweet cheeks," James said as he gave me a brief, but fond peck on the lips.

"Happy dreams, cute guy," I said as I returned his affectionate peck.

Moments later, I was snuggled down and dreaming. In this nocturnal excursion I was back in Manitoba, Canada. It was a cold winter night and I was sitting alone by a bonfire watching the flames. Before my very eyes, the shadows of these flames became the shadows of dancing Indians. The shadows departed and were soon replaced by another shadow, that of my lost love, Wayne. Then he was no longer a shadow, but a flesh and blood reality. Shortly, he was joined by his little Schnauzer dog, Checkers. I hugged them both. They were warm with love for me.

The next morning I found a sign from Wayne that he and his dog were both safe and happy in a heavenly realm and that they still loved me. It was a heart-shaped basalt rock with the name "Wayne" engraved on it. I found it in the snow bank the next morning when I left the Festiva to take me and Taffy out to pee. What made this volcanic rock truly unique was that its type is found in abundance in the small high prairie town of Goldendale, Washington where I first met spare, but spry, sweet-smiling Wayne Gresham. Never is it found in North Dakota.

Chapter Two

That morning, James came awake with a yawn and a stretch. Both Taffy and I had returned to the vehicle after our trip out to "drain the lilly", as Wayne would always put it. I had put the basalt rock in my purse.

"So how did you and your flying monkey sleep last night, circus cutie? All comfy, I hope," James asked as he kissed me on the cheek and then leaned over to turn the Festiva's heater on.

It would take a few minutes for the inside to heat up, since it had been gripped by a 30 minus temperature drop – typical North Dakota winter weather.

"We slept as snug as two bugs in a rug thanks to your wonderful down-filled blanket. So how'd you sleep, Mr. Muscles?" I asked smiling at his Wizard of Oz reference as I fed a peeled orange to Taffy.

She was sitting up with the blanket tucked in all around her.

"Slept fine. I even dreamed, which I don't usually do," James replied with another yawn.

"Interesting! What did you dream about, sweet guy?" I asked wanting to know every detail.

"Shadows."

"Isn't that something, so did I."

"Brilliant minds run in the same direction."

"Even in dreams?"

"Especially in dreams."

As I mulled that over in my mind, I put all of the blankets away and then settled myself down in my seat with Taffy as James prepared to back the vehicle out of its parking spot. We found we could not move. The snow drifts that had come down in the night had piled up so deep that the Festiva was hemmed in on all sides. The only way out was for both me and James to shovel us out. I was happy to do my share of the shoveling since I had grown up in northern Canada where the snow piles can reach arctic proportions.

James told me in a way that showed he was trying to be cheerful that he had two shovels with him and that both of us needed to get to work using them if we expected to make it to Dickinson any time soon. Eagerly, I took the one he offered me. It was mauve and he told me that it used to belong to "Lícia." Suddenly, I felt a pang of jealousy.

"Who's Lícia?" I asked, my voice carrying an acid tinge.

"My ex-wife. I'd rather not talk about her now. Right now, you and I need to focus on shoveling this car out!" said James in a slightly irritated tone as he grabbed his own shovel, a blue one, and set to work clearing a path.

Taking that as a cue, I forced my own emotions down and began to push the snow away from the little red car like I was a human snow plow. In minutes, a path was cleared and we were on our way through McKenzie to Bismarck.

James popped in another America CD and we were soon treated to the melodious sounds of the band's lead singer, Dan Peek, crooning "Sister Golden Hair." Even though my hair is auburn rather than golden like the girl in the song's lyrics, I still felt as though the tune applied directly to me and my present situation.

"I ain't ready for the alter, but I do agree there's times
When a woman can sure be a friend of mine."

These words from the soulful, mid-70s hit tune carried to me the direct meaning that to James Schönhausse I was that "woman." I was his "Sister Golden Hair." What's more, and as the song subtly implied, our friendship carried the building notes of something deeper and richer. Ours was a love song in the process of being composed and knowing that gave my spirits a much-needed lilt.

The CD continued playing and with each change of song, the scenery seemed to change too. The flat expanses of snowy field became rolling hills punctuated by clumps of trees. These trees were encrusted all over by hoarfrost that defined their branches and lent them a ghostly look. As we neared the bustling city of Bismarck, I saw increasing numbers of houses, some with barns and some standing alone. Many of these homes were of very old German design with shuttered windows and many gables. Some of them I guessed to have been built in the 1800s, some as early as the 1700s.

As the CD player accompanied us with America's "Don't Cross The River," we came to a bridge and went over The Apple River. Then we were on the edge of Bismarck.

"Don't cross the river if you can't swim the tide.
Don't try denyin' livin' on the other side."

Just then, the music ended and James pulled over to a truck stop called "The Wagon Wheel", which true to its name, had a sign in the form of a Conestoga wagon wheel.

"Well, this is it, m'dear. We can shower and have breakfast. Sound like a plan?" he announced as he led us into the rustic style building.

"Yes, Mr. Muscles, Taffy and I are starving and we both need to tidy up," I said as I gathered up my monkey and gave him a wink.

Very soon we found the showers. Before going into the shower room marked with a ten gallon hat and the words "Men's Showers" on the door, James gave me a kiss on the cheek. I returned his kiss and slipped into the room posted with a poke bonnet and a sign saying "Ladies Showers" with Taffy in my arms. Thankfully, the establishment was a pet-friendly one.

Enjoying the warmth of the shower cubicle, I disrobed and stepped into the shower stall with Taffy. Following our bath, I dried us off, dressed, and then touched up my hair a bit with my curling iron. I even put on a little make-up. Satisfied that Taffy and I were both fairly dolled-up, I gathered her in my arms and made my way over to where James was getting coffee from the coffee dispenser. I noticed that he had shaved and changed his shirt.

"Hi circus chick, you look gorgeous," he said softly as he handed me a cup of unsweetened coffee.

"Thank you, James. You look great this morning yourself. The highway becomes you," I said as I took the coffee and started sipping it slowly.

He got some coffee for himself and then led me and Taffy to The Wagon Wheel's eatery section. We found a booth under a portrait of Theodore Roosevelt, one of North Dakota's favorite sons, and sat down. Seconds later, a pretty waitress in a poke bonnet and ruffly pioneer dress came over to our booth with place mats and menus. She fussed over Taffy and then took our orders for a hearty breakfast of bacon, french toast, and more coffee. I included toast with jam and a cup of milk for the monkey.

As we waited for our order, James and I became engrossed in studying our place mats and what fascinating place mats they were. The paper they were printed on had been made to look like real buckskin and they were decorated with words and symbols related to the Lakota Sioux who are the predominant Indian tribe of the Dakotas, "Dakota" being their word for "friend".

"Look, it has the Lakota symbol for happy and the one for friendship," I said pointing at a stick figure with a heart in its center.

The symbol for friendship happened to be two crossed arrows.

"And here's the Cangleska, the Lakota symbol for the four sacred directions," said James as he drew my attention to a circle with a cross in its center which was made up of equal sections colored in red, white, black, and yellow.

Both of us commented on the various Lakota words and phrases that accompanied these and other symbols and pictographs. James has some background knowledge of the language and so was a big help to me as I learned about it. "Taŋyányahí", I discovered was this native peoples' word for "welcome."

At that moment, Miss poke bonnet returned with our food. We thanked her heartily and then set to eating it heartily. As we enjoyed our meal we continued to discuss the Lakotas and their language and mythos.

"These people have a legend about Ptesan Wi or the White Buffalo Woman, a female hero who was said to have brought them a magic pipe and taught them how to be civilized," James said, beginning one of his long dialogues, stopping just briefly to down the last of his coffee. But just as he was about to call Miss Poke Bonnet back to our table for another refill, who should blow in through the restaurant's door on the wild North Dakota wind than the same mysterious blond fellow we had given a ride to back at Curlew.

"Hi, friends. Boy howdy, is it cold out there!" announced the spare, white-clad man in a shivery, Midwestern twang.

Our hitch hiker had told us the day we picked him up that his name was "Adolf" and that he was a professional motorcycle racer and stunt master. At the moment we thought he might be the famous Adolf Geisst, but we knew that he could not be. Geisst had died the year before in a horrific, fiery accident during a motocross racing tournament.

While marveling at this coincidence in the backs of our minds we invited the thin, fair, stranger to come join us at our booth. With a relaxed smile, he sat down beside of James who ordered more coffee. I noticed that he was wearing a white beret with a silver motorcycle wheels pin along with a white wool trench coat, boots, and leather pants. Taffy reached for him with both hands and chittered. Adolf gave her his hat to play with, then he turned his attention to us humans.

"So, how goes it, Adolf? The last time we saw you was when we dropped you off by that gas station. You just stood there like a ghost," said James to our visitor, almost in jest.

For a moment, I thought I saw Adolf's pale features darken at the word "ghost", then he laughed.

"I had some business to square away that night. But I got it all done," he said almost flippantly.

"What'd it involve, my friend, money or motorcycles? Or

both?" asked James with amiable inquisitiveness.

"Let's just say it was about some unfinished business," replied Adolf with a look that had reticence written all over it.

Just then, our coffee arrived. Adolf accepted his with sugar and non-dairy creamer from a covered wagon-shaped dispenser on the table. Speaking for all three of us, James thanked our waitress and then returned his attention to our white-garbed friend.

"So how many bike races have you won lately?" my hefty companion asked as he looked into Adolf's icey blue eyes while sipping his coffee.

The stuntman-racer had gotten his beret back from Taffy and was holding it on his lap as he slowly savored his own coffee.

"Two – one in Silver City and one in Missoula," Adolf replied.

"Those are my old stomping grounds. Funny how people's paths can run parallel without actually crossing," said James with a hearty laugh.

"Yes, it truly is amazing how life and death work that way. So what were you doing in Silver City and Missoula?" now it was Adolf's turn to be curious.

"That was over ten years ago. And as to what I was doing, I was working for newspapers and trying to avoid my infamous brother, Maximilian, who as you well know has also made a name for himself as a motocross racer and stunt rider," said James and I could tell by his face that he was holding a lot back concerning his time in Silver City.

"I don't avoid him, I challenge him."

14

"Have you raced against the asshole lately?"

"Yes, and I plan to again this fall. We are slated to compete with each other in a jumping match here at Sentinel Butte."

"Sounds exciting, Adolf. What will you and your nemesis be riding your bikes over up there?" I chimed in with genuine interest as Taffy played with a lock of my hair.

"Ha ha! Maximilian Schön is not my nemesis. He's not even fit to eat the dust I leave as I zoom past him. He's a jackass in leathers who gets lucky sometimes, but I usually beat him. I'll beat him again this coming October when we take a spin over the saddle there at Sentinel Butte," said Adolf as he glanced from me to James.

James was grinning at the thought of someone besting his egocentric brother.

"Good for you. I'll enjoy seeing you make that grand leap across the Sentinel Butte saddle this autumn.

"They've found some really interesting fossils there, ones from the Paleocene Era," remarked James who really did not like talking for very long about his younger brother.

And when I thought of everything he had told me about the living hell "Max" had put him through as they were growing up together, I really didn't blame him.

"They've found a lot of prehistoric ginko tree leaves and the fossils of fish and turtles," I added, my own interest in geology and paleontology having been sparked by my past explorations of the stony area.

"Not to mention the remains of the bear-like Titanoides and the Champsosaurus, one of the ancestors of the modern crocodile,"

15

said James, bringing in his own knowledge of paleontology to give depth to the discussion.

"Chuckle. I never was much into dinosaurs as a kid, so all that stuff is out of my league. My first and only love was always motorcycles. I rode behind my dad on one practically from birth. Then I learned to ride when I was 13. Got my own, a second hand Harley, when I was 15. Rode it all across the Great Lakes Region in the summer of '73," confessed our bike-racing friend with a touch of understandable pride.

"I have a love-hate relationship with motorcycles, because along with the steel horse road trips and encounters with outlaw bikers I've enjoyed, there's also that bad accident I had on one back in 1982 in Silver City. I've had uneasy feelings about both motorcycles and Silver City ever since," revealed James with a tinge of sadness.

As I learned later, this accident not only gave him a skull fracture and a brain-flooding with blood, but also a spinal injury and a temporary case of epilepsy.

"I know, James," said Adolf slowly and with emphasis. "I know all about your accident."

"How do you know about it? Were you there?" James asked as he locked his light-brown eyes with Adolf's icey blue eyes in a gaze that was meant to be a penetrating search for truth.

"Let's just say, friends, that I was and that I helped out. I can't say any more right now because I need to go and meet with my agent to talk over some contracts I need to sign. Racing and stunt cycling have their business side, you know," said Adolf as he deftly dodged James' verbal parries.

He then stood up and prepared to leave, downing the last of his coffee.

"Here's a little thanks for your kind company on a cold morning," said Adolf as he handed James another couple $100 bills.

Then he did something surprising and sweet. He removed the silver pin from his beret and gave it to Taffy.

"A little trinket for your monkey," he said as I took it from her and pinned it on her jacket.

"Thanks, Adolf. It's cute as a button," I said beaming.

"The monkey and I both thank you," chimed in James as he shook Adolf's hand.

I shook his hand in turn. At the moment I released the stunt biker's firm hand, Taffy reached over and grasped it.

"It was fun seeing you again, Adolf. It's interesting how we ran into each other again. Like fate or something was determined that we meet the second time and at the least expected moment," said James in a way that was reflective, but casual too.

"The Sioux call it Maya Owicha Paka," I added with a bright smile.

"Back in Nebraska we just call it a good old fashioned coincidence," said Adolf as he let go of the little monkey and put on his beret.

"Whatever you call it, Adolf, it all amounts to one thing. Life itself brings people together who are meant to be friends, but sometimes obstacles keep getting in the way. That's why some people keep bumping into each other repeatedly," said James as he put the money in the chained wallet he always wore attached to his leather belt.

"I just know our paths will cross again sometime soon," Adolf said as he favored all three of us with a smile and headed for the restaurant's door.

A second later, his tall, angular form went out The Wagon Wheel's door, or did he just vanish through it in a sudden blur of white? Was it real or was it Memorex?

Chapter Three

James paid for our breakfast and then we were back in his car and on our way into the throbbing heart of the city of Bismarck. By that time, it was nearing the noon hour. We drove past the lofty, white, State Capitol Building with its art deco contours and snow-covered statues – one of them of Sakakawea – reknown lady guide of Lewis and Clark. On the way to Arrowhead Plaza, we also passed by the historic Cathedral District, so-called because of its famous art deco church. This neighborhood was very distinctive also because of its narrow streets, lofty elm trees, and houses that were built in the 1800s and early Twentieth Century.

In minutes, we arrived at Arrowhead Plaza, a white triple box structure with square pillars and a mottled-looking gray cement parking lot with patches of snow here and there. After parking, James and I went to Dan's Supervalu to buy much-needed supplies. As we were checking out, the grocery clerk, who was a young blond boy, fussed over Taffy and gave her a banana.

After putting our goods in the back, we were on our way again through the city that was first called "Mirahaci Arumaaquash" or "Place of the Tall Willows" by the Mandan Indians who were its first inhabitants. On the outskirts of the city, we had a brief lunch at Fort Lincoln State Park, former headquarters of General Custer's 7th Cavalry. When we were done the three of us went on a tour of the nearby On Slant Village, home of the rebuilt Mandan earth lodge mounds. These Indian dwellings were round piles of earth with square wooden doorways. After taking a few photographs we got back in James' car and were on Interstate 94 headed west.

As we traveled along, we talked about our mysterious bike-rider friend. We decided together that he really was the famous Adolf "Addy" Geisst the motocross champion and daredevil who had saved Jame's life back in 1982. For some reason, he had faked his own death and was now hiding out, we were certain of that. However, we decided not to press him into revealing his secrets, if and when we ever met him again.

"He'll tell us when he's ready," explained James as he squinted at the receding prairie sun.

It was getting to be night fall.

"Could be he's hiding from your brother," I quipped half-seriously.

We talked some more in this vein as we headed into the town of New Salem. Soon, we were greeted by the sight of Salem Sue, an enormous plexiglass Holstein cow that stood on the hills over looking the small city.

"We've got the world's largest Holstein cow that looks across our fields. Her presence shows that New Salem grows with milk-producer's yields,"

James and I sang this town anthem together as we passed by the 38 foot faux bovine and headed onto main street. Both of us had become acquainted with this dairy town's signature ditty during earlier travels in the area.

We noted that the streets on both sides were lined with stores that were modern enough but had Old West-style flat, squarish fronts. James and I stopped briefly at one, a clothing shop, and bought suits and shoes. After all, we had an interview coming up the next day.

By then it was getting late and time for us to check into a motel. In addition, the wind was starting to pick up and snow clouds were gathering in the darkening sky above. A blizzard was on its way.

Driving a little ways further down Main Street, we found The Arrowhead Inn, a solid green, white, and red brick structure. After checking in, we lost no time in unloading our vehicle and settling into our cozy room with its homespun decor and paintings of Prairie Schooners. Outside, the wind and snow hit with all of the fury that Old Father Winter can muster.

Very tired from our travels, we had a light supper and then prepared to bed down for the night. First, I used the bathroom to change into my nightie, then James went in there and put on his pajamas which more resembled gym clothes than men's regular night wear. There happened to be two beds. James hunkered down in one, while I tucked the already sleeping Taffy into the one beside him and prepared to join her. James, however, had other ideas.

"Come in here and keep me warm tonight, circus chick," he said invitingly as he threw back the covers of his bed on one side.

Filled with calm joy at his invitation, I slipped in beside my handsome muscular companion and snuggled close.

"Good night, sweet cheeks," said James softly as he gave me a brief, but affectionate kiss on the lips and wrapped his arm around me pulling me even closer.

"Sweet dreams, cute guy," I said as I softly returned James' kiss and then cuddled down into the solid warmth of his arms and fell asleep to the rhythm of his heart beat.

All we did that night was snuggle close while the wind and snow pounded the windows and outside walls of the motel fiercely. I never felt so blissfully happy or complete.

It wasn't long before I started to dream. It was winter in Goldendale, Washington and I was back in the tan, two story house that I once shared with Wayne Gresham. We were sitting at his big wooden kitchen table drinking his espressos and watching the snowflakes fall blissfully through the air while Checkers cuddled in my lap. We were chatting about everything and nothing as we usually did every morning, any time of the year, then he reached over and lovingly grasped my hand.

Wayne, honey, how come you never married me?" I asked him in a voice full of hurt.

"I realize now that I should have. But I didn't because of your brother. I was afraid that if I married you he would get you to divorce me and rip off all of my assets. I realize now how wrong I was to believe that he could," replied Wayne whose face showed how repentant he was feeling.

I forgave him and squeezed his hand fondly. Wayne's fears had not been entirely unfounded. My brother, Alan, could be very domineering and meddling. Still, he couldn't have coerced me into betraying the man I loved and I was glad to see that Wayne understood that now, finally. Still, there were other issues between us that needed, no, demanded to be addressed.

"I'm so sorry for all of the times I cheated on you, Wayne," I said as I turned away from him and buried my face in my hands.

I started sobbing. Outside, the falling snow was drifting harder.

"I forgave you for that a long time ago. I feel that I drove you to those other men with my bad temper, my stinginess, and the fact that I wouldn't marry you. You're the one who needs to forgive me," he said as he pulled his chair closer to mine and hugged me.

"I do, Wayne honey, I do. But why did you die and leave me so suddenly? I never got a chance to tell you goodbye. That really traumatized me," I said as he released me but kept his arm across my shoulders.

Checkers jumped down and sat at our feet pensively all eyes and ears.

"Yes, my queen, I know how grievous my death was for you and then little Checkers died on top of all that. But I had to go sudden like that. You see, God called me up to Heaven to help someone, to give guidance to someone whom He was going to outfit for a great mission on Earth as well as here in Heaven," explained Wayne as he stared at me with his blue eyes full of wisdom and compassion.

"Who were you taken up to help? Who on Earth could have been that important?" I asked, a little stunned at realizing that I was in Heaven myself.

I gathered Checkers up in my arms and held her close. Could I have died too?

"No, my queen, you are very much alive. And no, I can't tell you who I was called up to help, at least not yet. Revealing his identity too soon to anyone who is still living could spoil the success of his holy mission. Now, you must go back to the realm of the living. But rest assured, Checkers and I still love you and we're watching out for you," Wayne, who had read my thoughts, promised me as he kissed me deeply on the mouth.

Checkers licked me on the cheek. Then they and the house melted away like snow in the bright sunlight that was beaming into my eyes through a crack in the motel room's drapes. It was early morning. Outside the sun was shining in spite of the frosty cold still air and the huge mounds of snow that had piled up on everything over night.

I awoke in James' arms feeling more refreshed and happy than I'd felt in a long while. He kissed me on the cheek and then we both took turns showering, grooming, and putting on our brand-new suits and shoes, our minds on the big interview that was coming up at 10:00 am that day at *The Dickinson Ledger* news-paper office.

As I was taking my crisp, well-tailored lady's suit out of its package, a piece of paper fluttered out of it. Curious, I picked it up and gave it a closer look. On that 3 by 2½ inch square of white paper were the shadow-like silhouettes of a man and a dog. I recognized them instantly – it was Wayne and Checkers. I kissed the Heaven-sent memento and then put it in my Bible.

"Thank you, God," I said to myself blissfully. "Death is nothing to fear. It is only a shadow of the light to come, the light of Heaven."

Chapter Four

When I was fully dressed, I took care of Taffy's needs. Then James had us get into his little car and we were on our way to the Muddy River Coffee House for breakfast.

"Bonnie, you always look nice, but today in your new suit and shoes you look positively gorgeous. You will do well on your interview, I'm sure of that," said James with a sweet smile as he took the wheel.

"Thank you, James, and you look quite the handsome professional yourself in your brand new suit and shoes," I said, happy to return his compliment and he did indeed look really sharp that day, like a man who had truly "dressed for success."

He thanked me with a wink and in a few minutes we were in the snowbank enclosed parkway of the gray and white ranch-style, Muddy River Coffee House. Because the eating establishment was not, unfortunately, a pet friendly one, we had to leave Taffy behind in the Festiva. Of course, we made sure that she was well-bundled up and pacified with an apple before we left her for the white wooden steps leading up into the large rustic building. I noticed that pine branch garlands entwined the length of the steps and rails. Definitely leftovers from the Christmas holiday.

Once inside, we found a table and ordered a breakfast of sausages, waffles, and coffee – lots of plain coffee. Out of concern for Taffy, we ate hurriedly and saved some bites for her. We washed down our meal and were back in James' vehicle, headed for Dickinson or "Mayberry on the Prairie" as it is often called. Taffy munched on the bits of buttered pancake we shared with her. All during the half hour drive, I was very anxious about the impending newspaper interview, but James assured me that I would do just fine. He advised me to focus, present myself honestly and in the most positive light, and to not forget to show the person doing the interview my newspaper article from *The Caribou Bugle*.

Luckily, I always carried in my handbag an article that I had written for that weekly paper. It was about one of the Canadian town's most prominent pioneer families, The Moffats, who had rolled over from Manitoba to British Columbia in an ox driven covered wagon in 1833. I had even embellished the article with my own drawings, photographs, and poetry. I carried the clipping with me always as a matter of pride and James let me know that it would be an ideal resume for me since it was, in his opinion, well-written and well-illustrated. Plus, its topic would appeal to most North Dakotans who had similar pioneer heritages. All I would need, he told me, would be my ID card to prove I was who I said I was and that I was the actual author of the article and my credentials would be complete. Like any other sensible person, I had an ID card with me too.

James and I took turns briefing each other for the interview, as we rolled past seemingly borderless snowy fields which were broken now and then by clumps of trees, castle-like pillars of sandstone, and the occasional farm. On our way, we passed through the small town of Richardson where, James explained, one could find all kinds of arrow heads. He promised to take me and Taffy back there someday when the weather was better and all three of us could go hunting for them. I beamed as I told him that was something I really looked forward to doing.

A few minutes later and we were in the bustling oil and agri-culture rich city of Dickinson. I took Taffy out for a potty break at a local park restroom and seconds later we arrived at the large brown brick Dickinson Ledger newspaper building that housed the offices as well as the printing presses. As punctual as James was, we were right on time. As I left her in the car and followed James through the Ledger's revolving door into the waiting room, I told myself not to be nervous, but I still was – very. We did not have long to wait, however. Just as James and I found some overstuffed chairs in the waiting lounge we were met by a doughy-faced, but personable middle-aged blonde woman who introduced herself as Marian Aylmer, the paper's Managing Editor and the person who would be doing our interviews. Ms. Aylmer further explained that the two of us would be interviewed separately in order to avoid confusion and so that our individual talents could be assessed better.

First, James was directed into her office and she closed the door. For a while, I sat nervously in the waiting room trying to get interested in an *Allure* fashion magazine. Thirty minutes later, I gave into the urge to go over to Ms. Aylmer's closed door and eavesdrop. What I heard delighted me no end. I clearly heard Ms. Aylmer's voice say, "You're hired, Mr. Schönhausse." And I also caught him telling her that I was his "girlfriend" and that I was "highly intelligent as well as beautiful."

Elated, I resumed my seat and pretended to read a *Time* magazine. Seconds later, James was out the door with a smile bigger than a Dickinson farm field.

"Good news, circus chick, I've been hired on as a journalist and I'll be doing feature
writing. Now its your turn. Go in there and make me proud," he said as I stood up from my chair and gave him a congratulatory hug.

"That is good news, cute guy. I'm so proud of you and I feel that I will do well at this interview. But wish me luck," I said as I released him and headed into the Managing Editor's office.

He told me that I couldn't "lose for winning" as I left him and sat down in front of Ms. Aylmer's wooden desk. In an amiable, but professional voice she asked me a few questions about my education, former jobs, and current goals. When I showed her the *Caribou Bugle* clipping, it was the deal clincher. She looked it over while nodding her head, very pleased. She handed it back to me and informed me that I was hired for the position I craved – that of Poetry Editor. After telling me to report in for work the next morning, she shook my hand and I left her office feeling like I was walking on fluffy clouds.

The moment I was back again with James in the lobby, I told him what had just transpired. Feeling elated for both of us, he told me that he never doubted I would succeed in the interview. To further congratulate me, he put his arm over my shoulders and led me out to his little red Festiva. To celebrate our success, James told me with an impish grin, he was going to give me and Taffy a special treat. He was going to escort us through the big city of Dickinson, North Dakota.

For the rest of the day and well into the night, we would ride high on "The Western Edge" of that prairie metropolis. First of all, James treated me to lunch at The Wurst Place In Dickinson. As its name implied, it was a German restaurant where the food was excellent and the decor was colorfully rural. The place didn't allow pets, so we ate quickly. Just before leaving, we ordered a stuffed, seasoned potato just for Taffy. As she munched on her potato, we took her with us on a tour that included The Dickinson Museum Center, with its impressive dinosaur and gem and mineral exhibits, the Ukranian Cultural Institute, The Dickinson State University Art Gallery, and The Pioneer Machinery building. We topped off our jaunt with a visit to a Mandan Indian reservation where we were privileged to view basket weavers at their craft and a sacred smuge-burning ceremony. Before leaving, I bought three cobs of parti-colored indian corn. I felt that by making that purchase, I had somehow lifted a heavy veil of misfortune from both James' life and mine. Especially since the tribal Shaman, who was as endearingly wizened as an apple doll, left us with a blessing,

"May you walk in beauty,
   May your eyes ever behold the red and golden sunset,
   May you learn the lessons Great Spirit has
   Hidden in every rock and fossil bed,
   Seek strength, not to be greater
   Than your brothers and sisters,
   But to fight your greatest enemy,
   The enemy within ourselves."

Spoke the twinkly-eyed Shaman as he shook his rattle over us while James held my hand fondly and I held Taffy. By then it was supper time, so we left our Mandan adventure for further adventures at the rough and rowdy Spur Bar and Lounge. We had our meal and then got up and did some lively line dancing. The management let us bring Taffy in with us and she quickly stole the show when the line dancing was done and she did a little solo dance to the tune of my accordion. All three of us left a little tipsy that night. Even Taffy whom I let have a small amount of beer.

We weren't too tipsy though to have the sense to check into a Best Western Motel before the wee hours of the night. James checked the three of us into the pet-friendly establishment, while telling the fellow at the desk, who was obviously part Mandan, that I was his "girlfriend". The man gave us a knowing smile, while I felt my feelings of self-worth rise to new heights. But just as James was about to hand the desk clerk the $135 room fee in return for the key, who should walk over to us then Adolf, our white knight in shining leather.

"That's all right man. I'll pay for your accommodations here," he said in his Nebraskan twang as he handed $135 in bills to the surprised desk clerk and grinned "Hello" at me and James.

We both thanked him heartily as James took the key for Room 82. Before going to find it we chatted with Adolf for a few minutes. Then he told us he had to go, but he was happy to see us again. As a parting gift, he gave James $1000 in one hundred dollar bills.

"What's that for, Addy?" James asked, his broad face showing both delight and puzzlement.

"For a down payment on a house when you find one here," he answered as he gave Taffy a loving pat.

"But I have a job now."

"That don't matter. It'll come in handy for something for you and your girls."

Then with a smile, he was gone. But where oh where did our lanky friend disappear to?

As James pocketed the wad of Ben Franklins, we both smiled and shrugged our shoulders at each other. Then we were off to find Room 82. When we found the apartment's door, James unlocked it and did an unexpected and delightful thing. He scooped me up in his powerful arms and carried me in, monkey and all.

"Make yourself to home, sweet cheeks, and your little monkey too," he purred in my ear as he gently set me down on the room's smooth tan carpeting.

On cue, I put Taffy to bed on the suite's living room couch, then I joined James who was waiting for me in the bedroom with an eager smile. He kissed me, not with a bashful peck but with a deep, open-mouthed kiss of strong, but gentle passion.

"I love you, Bonnie," he told me as he picked me up and laid me tenderly on the king-sized bed.

A moment later, our clothes were strewn all over the floor and James and I were making hot, passionate love. After our libidinous romp, I fell asleep in my beefy boyfriend's husky arms, feeling that my life was at last happy, truly happy.

That night I dreamed happy too. I was back in Goldendale with Wayne walking along the trail in Ekone Park as Checkers scampered along beside us. This primitive parkland lay just outside the town's limits and one-quarter of a mile from the home he and I once shared.

As we climbed out of the woods and onto the meadow clearing with The Little Klickitat River gurgling past us the whole way, I noticed that my beloved was dressed in a soccer player's uniform and was carrying a soccer ball. How splendid he looked in spite of or because of his seventy-plus years. Just then a handsome youth of about 15 with light-brown eyes and hair and an impish grin came onto the clearing path from the woods on the opposite end. He too was wearing a soccer player's outfit. As I returned the young man's smile, I thought of how much he resembled James. Wayne tossed him the soccer ball.

"Here you are, son. She's all yours now. Take good care of her," he said as the tawny-haired boy caught the ball.

"I will, sir," promised the youth with Boy Scout-like earnestness.

At that moment, Wayne and Checkers began to fade into the verdant shadows of the forest. I cried out to them, but Wayne with his beautiful dog in his arms waved "goodbye". Before being absorbed completely into the trees, bushes, moss, and wildflowers, he lifted her little paw in a farewell gesture. Then they were both gone completely. I sat down on a nearby pine stump and started to weep hard.

I was not to remain disconsolate for long, however. The teenaged soccer player came over to me and took me by the hand in a playfully romantic way. At the touch of his hand I felt myself change back into a 14-year-old girl. We walked down the woodsy park trail laughing and taking turns bouncing the ball. As we neared the clump of woods where the wild purple irises grew we were holding hands and I was singing a ballad I had just composed in my heart.

"I had a date with a handsome soccer player,
His arms were so strong they amazed my eyes,
I asked him for this ballgame
And then he obliged me,
Was I surprised, yeah,
Was I surprised,
No not at all."

On that cheery note, I awoke to the sounds and smells of James in the kitchen part of the suite making German potato pancakes. I also smelled brewing coffee. As I got up and stretched I happened to glance over at my pillow. Beside it was a photograph of a young boy in a soccer player's uniform kneeling with a soccer ball. He looked exactly like the brown-eyed boy in my dream.

With a smile in my heart that reached down into my soul I took the photograph and joined James who was busy at the stove in his gym suit/pajamas flipping the pancakes.

"Good morning, Bonnie m'dear," he said as he looked at me from the corner of his eye and smiled.

I walked over and showed him the photo I'd found.

"Good morning to you, cute guy. Now tell me who this fine-looking young soccer player is," I asked almost sure of what his answer would be.

"Ha ha. That's me, Bonnie love. I was quite the jock, wasn't I?" James commented blithely as he scooped up the last pancake he was frying onto a tall stack with the others. Those pgann-kuchen (pancakes) smelled divine.

"You still are," I said as I hugged him from behind and kissed him on the neck.

James enjoyed my display of affection. I could tell by the way he returned my kiss on my mouth.

Chapter Five

On our first morning together as a loving couple in Dickinson, North Dakota, James made breakfast, while I set the table and little Taffy who had slept in, watched on while chattering merrily. During our breakfast, James explained his deep affection for all things German and where he had learned to fry such delicious pfannkuchen.

"It was from my mother, Jenell, she was German right to the back bone. Her maiden name was Webber. My father, Martin, was German too, with some Swiss mixed in," explained James between mouthfuls of pancake.

"That's another thing we have in common, James, because I've got German on both sides of my family. My great-grandfather, Hanns-Dolphus Von Bär, was a Hessian Soldier during the American Revolutionary War. He came right from Stuttgart. Those Hessians were mercenaries who'd hire on to fight for either side and grandpa chose the American side. But along with German, my family also has some English, French, and Irish mixed in," I added as I sipped my coffee.

"Fascinating ethnic mixture, m'dear. I know the French. I met some French Army guys when I was in the Army and stationed in what was then West Germany. That was during some joint NATO troop maneuvers," continued James as he carved up another pancake. Between us, Taffy was busy eating her share, but with orange juice in a small plastic mug rather than coffee.

"Just where in West Germany were you stationed, cute guy?" I asked, my eyes wide with interest.

"Fulda Gap, also known as 'the armpit of Europe'."

"Come now, it was a region important to the defense of the whole continent at the time."

"Indeed it was, Circus Chick, but that mountain ridged valley was still the hardest duty station in Europe. We were in the field all the time and in every kind of weather."

"I know it must have been rough, but I'll bet you have some happy memories of the country as well. I think of the mountains, the beer, the music."

"Yes, on my off duty times I enjoyed it all. I even went skiing once in the Alps with one of my Army buddies. I was a part of the 11th Cavalry. My MOS was demolitions and I worked my way up to Corporal."

"You had quite an exciting life over there, James love. Thank you for your service," I said as I kissed him on the mouth.

James returned my kiss and then glanced at his watch.

"It's 8:30 am and time for us to get ready for work. Big day ahead, you know," announced my little Corporal.

On that signal, he left to shower, shave, and spruce up in his suit. While he was getting ready, I did the dishes, wiped the table, and fixed us both a bagged lunch of a tuna sandwich, a banana, and a bag of Fritos. I also threw in an extra banana for Taffy, since I'd been told by Ms. Alymer that it would be okay for us to bring her.

When it was my turn to pretty up, I showered and followed

this up by using my curling iron and putting on make-up and nail polish. Of course, I put on my own suit as well. Taffy, who'd showered with me, I toweled off, brushed out, and dressed in a fresh little outfit.

"You look lovely, Bonnie sweet cheeks," said James in a deep tender voice the moment he saw me coming out the restroom door.

I thanked him and told him he looked marvelous. Then the three of us were out the door and in his red car headed for *The Dickinson Ledger* office in the heart of the imposing, history-laden city.

Once we were through the door, the Chief Editor, Mike Lazarenko, welcomed each of us with a handshake and directed me and James to our cubicles. Then he left us to get right to work. We each knew just what needed to be done. James wasted no time in looking over lists of potential interviewees and contacting them by phone and e-mail, while I perused a stack of poems by local people and prepared them for publication.

To the delight of the other newspaper staff I had Taffy helping me with simple tasks like handing me papers and pressing certain buttons on my desk top computer. Even though our cubicles were practically side by side, James and I never distracted each other. We were both determined, focused people who loved the work we were doing. When lunch time came we nibbled on our bagged sandwiches and kept on with the tasks at hand, while the rest of the staff sat, ate, and chatted in the company lunch room. At 2:00 pm, James left the building to go to a meeting of the local grange since one of his journalistic duties was to do articles about the area's farms and agriculture.

"As a teenager in Utah I often did work on farms and ranches. I was even a cowboy then. So all of that farm stuff is second nature to me," James told me with a satisfied smile when he returned to his cubicle with a rough draft of the farm report in hand.

"And I grew up on a farm in the Canadian Rockies, so that's familiar territory to me too," I reminded him as I returned his smile and then continued reading a poem titled "My Homestead In Winter."

James and I continued to focus and work hard and at the end of the day with the shadows of 6 pm gathering about the city outside, he had seven articles ready and I had, with some assistance from Taffy, a whole page of poems done. Mr. Lazarenko was very pleased and told us so.

We took some of our tasks home with us that first work day evening. James wanted to finish an article he'd started about a local veteran of World War One, while I had a bundle of poems to edit and contribute one of my own to. We enjoyed a brief supper that I hastily, but tastily put together and then I put Taffy to bed before attacking my pile of poetry. James, meanwhile, soldered himself to perfecting his article. By 11 o'clock we were both done. Stimulated, rather than exhausted by all that paperwork, James and I got ready for bed and then made vigorous, ardent love in the suite's brown quilt-covered, king-sized bed.

"I love you, Bonnie," said James drowsily when we were both satisfied and lying in the embrace of requited ardor.

Then he kissed me and dozed off. I soon fell asleep to in the warmth and strength of his loving arms. I found myself in a wintry North Dakota dreamscape. I was at a farm like the one I saw when me and my beefy companion were driving through Crystal Springs, South Dakota. That farm had a unique windmill with shadow figure ornaments that danced with each other around and around as the wind blew them. They were done in the likenesses of a bride and groom. This metal bridal couple also made shadows on the winter hardened ground. Shadows of shadows. For me this dream was the happy herald of domestic and career bliss to come. I awoke the next morning with a giggle, feeling like I was in Heaven.

Truly, for me and James, life had taken a turn for the better ever since we arrived in Dickinson, North Dakota. Every week day morning, he and I took turns making breakfast and a bagged lunch. Then grabbing Taffy, we'd hurry off to another fulfilling day at the office. James would dedicate himself to conducting interviews and writing articles, while I, equally dedicated, would focus on my poetry section. As we kept on working hard and excelling at our jobs, we were each entrusted with more responsibilities that brought with them chances for promotion.

In February, James was given the added responsibility of laying out the entire newspaper and supervising its publication every Monday. Usually that was Mr. Lazarenko's job. At this same time, I was placed in charge of The Ledger's lifestyle column whenever its regular Editor, Patsy Belfield, needed to go on vacation or take a break. I always embellished this column with an original poem or a picture of Taffy.

Once a day, when one of us would leave our cubicle, James and I further showed our love and devotion by leaving little treats for each other on our desks. For me, There would always be a love poem with a flower. Likewise, I would leave a poem for James and sweeten it by including a home baked cookie.

Serious news people that we were, not a day went by that we didn't take our unfinished journalistic business home with us. Often, we both did overtime at the office. It only goes without saying that because of our efforts, *The Dickinson Ledger*, which was already a popular paper, began to increase its circulation even more. Mr. Lazarenko, being the good boss that he was, paid us each $22 an hour and told us we had good futures in the company.

Sometimes, James and I would go out for supper or have a meal brought in if we were working late. Usually, we would eat at the motel where we were booked for an extended stay. James and I would take turns making supper. Often, we would prepare it together. But although I love to cook, I must confess that James is the better all around cook and baker. He would frequently surprise me with mouth-watering gourmet dishes for our supper.

So we would always set to work on our homework, so to speak, on a full stomach. We would diligently apply ourselves to the jobs assigned to us by our Editor, but we would always be finished by 11 pm.

Then we would jump into bed and wear the mattress out making love. It was just like that sweet ballad, "Best of My Love", by our other favorite 70s smooth rock band, The Eagles.

"Oh, sweet darlin,'
  You get the best of my love,
  Every night and day,
  You get the best of my love."

On the weekends our schedule was different. Come Saturday mornings, we would attend the local Seventh Day Adventist Church because that's where our religious roots were anchored the deepest. Afterwords, we would take in the museums and the Mandan "Rez". Every Sunday, we made a beeline for these same and similar locales. When suppertime rolled around, we headed for the saucy Spur Bar And Lounge where we dined, drank, and line-danced until the bright lights were fading to blue, to paraphrase another Eagles hit, "Take It To The Limit".

James and I truly were taking it to the limit every weekend. However, we were prudent enough to settle down and sober up come Monday.

As the snow receded and merrybells and wild geranium blossoms began to grace the greening prairies, James and I soon had more weekend activities to enjoy. We camped out at Theodore Roosevelt National Park and went for hikes on its grassy trails. We hunted fossils in the Badlands and marveled at the area's tall pillared sandstone rock structures. We went on urban archaeological digs, that is, James and I dug out at the ruins of former outhouses, middens, and other such sites. It was amazing some of the things we found. People in times past would throw everything from bottles to money down those two-holers. Of course, we went arrowhead hunting at Richardton.

Just about everywhere James and I went, we took Taffy with us. When some place wasn't pet-friendly, we left her with a monkey sitter. By that time we could afford one with all of the money we were making.

Now and then we met up with Addy and chatted with him awhile. But he never stayed long and he stopped handing us money. This was wise since not only did we no longer need it, but he was obviously investing most of his time and cash in the stunt jump he would be doing in October. James and I were really looking forward to watching that, especially if he out-jumped Maximilian Schön.

James, being the fitness enthusiast that he was soon found a gym to work out in. He even began preparing to take part in national weight-lifting competitions. I joined too and worked out with him. To my delight and surprise, I found I could lift heavier weights than I thought I was capable of.

Of course, James and I bought a house of our own and moved into it. This was a three story, gabled, brown and yellow, old German structure. It had a broad staircase and 20 rooms. James and I furnished each one with a different theme. There was a Mandan Room splendid with Indian rugs, feathers, snake and coyote skins, and pottery. There was also a German Room and a

Theodore Roosevelt Room, to name a few examples.

With this new house as an added bonus I felt my life was heading on an upward swing that nothing could stop or slow down. Things were going that way and seemed like they would stay that way.

Chapter Six

Than came the last days in May when wildflowers dotted the state park, forest, wetland, and prairie landscapes in beautiful hues of purple, blue, red, pink, yellow, and orange. It was also around this time that James and I viewed the small but proud Memorial Day Parade and the rousing flag raising ceremony that followed at the local cemetery. During this summery celebration twin of Veteran's Day, James reminded everyone we met of his Army Fulda Gap days and his days with the Eagle Scouts in Layton, Utah. This seemed fitting since both the Army and the Boy Scouts were well-represented in the parade.

Things were going happily for us and it appeared they would stay that way. Then on May 31st, James and I were called one by one into Mr. Lazarenko's office for some dire news.

"Ms. Barry," said the Editor-in-Chief as he fixed me with a serious, almost accusatory stare with his beetling-browed blue eyes, "because you did time in Yakima State Mental Hospital for attempted suicide and were given psychiatric medication, I must let you go. I will not tolerate the reputation of my newspaper being besmirched by having a lunatic on my staff."

What could I do? Speechless, I left his office in tears. When James saw me, he hugged me and tried to tenderly console me, saying that he would vouch for me when he spoke with the Editor. Then it was his turn to go into the now ominous main office. As I waited sobbing in the lobby, I heard raised angry voices, but was too distraught to make out any words.

A few minutes later, James was out of the room slamming the door behind him, his broad handsome face ruddy with rage.

"They found out!" he said in a deep angry tone of voice that sounded like thunder.

"A-about what, James?" I stammered.

"The felony conviction! Come on, Bonnie, we're outta here. I'll tell you all about it at home," he fumed as he took me by the hand and led me out of our now former place of employment.

We drove home in silence, ate a brief supper, and then spent the night in the red and gold German Room, which we were drawn to as the most comforting at that time. As we sat close to each other on the picturesque chamber's yellow gold divan cradling Taffy between us, James and I revealed secrets that were so painful we'd kept them hidden even from ourselves. While above us an oaken cuckoo clock and photos of my robust boyfriend from his Fulda Gap days looked on as silent witnesses as we made these tearful confessions.

"It all started when I moved to Silver City, New Mexico," James began somberly. "I settled there in 1977 because I liked the climate and the educational opportunities it offered. I'd just gotten out of the service and was looking for a fresh new way to reinvent myself. What's more, I'd been jilted by Leah, my fiance´, and that was another reason I was eager to put my whole past behind me.

"After enrolling at Western New Mexico University, it wasn't long before I was hired as an investigative journalist by *The Silver City Sun*. I even got a new girlfriend. She was a Mexican chick named Leandra. We took the same history, grammar, and poetry classes together.

"Every aspect of my life was on the way up and rising higher,

then I made my first mistake. Leandra and I shared a side interest in archaeology and were particularly drawn to The Gila Cliff
Dwellings that had been built in 1275 by the ancient Mimbres
Mogolon Indians. They preceded the Apaches by hundreds of
years.

"Anyway, one hot summer night we were drawn to that rock
enclosed building site too much and with the wrong intentions.
She dared me to climb up there and steal a clay marriage jar that
we had seen up there during a university sponsored tour along
with some cobs of Indian corn. And silly, amorous fellow that I
was then I leaped up the crumbling stone steps to retrieve these
objects like the boy in the German poem 'Rose Red' who fell to
his death while trying to pluck a rose from a mountaintop for his
girlfriend. And all for a kiss."

"How romantic," I interposed, "even if you were stealing and
trespassing."

"Romantic, yes. But oh what foolish and harmful deeds
are often done in the name of romance," James said with sad
wisdom, then he resumed his tableau.

"When I brought down the jar and corn cobs, we compounded
our sin by taking them to a nearby mesa, building a fire, and
using the jar to pop the corn in. What a grand party we had
that night eating popcorn and making love under the full moon.
My dreams, however, convicted me of the gravity of my wrong
doing. In the first one, a gila monster blocked my way snarling
at the very entrance to the ruins that were its namesake. In the
second one, Silver City's famous Kneeling Nun rock formation
came alive and spoke to me with dire warnings and accusations.

"I awoke the next morning to find my girlfriend gone. She
left behind her colorful shawl from Mazatlán, Mexico, the city
where she was born. With feelings of crushing loneliness and
with Leandra's scarf in hand, I returned to Silver City.

"From that night of dubious, stolen pleasure on, my life began a downward spiral and so did Leandra's. First, she broke up with me, then I learned that she had taken her life by throwing herself down from the cliffs we had defiled. Although a cousin who was with her that night swears she was pushed by someone or something unseen.

"That was wrenching enough, but even worse was yet to come. I started to notice in my role as a reporter that the whole Silver City legal system was one rotten rat's nest. Through tip-offs from inside sources and my own sleuthing, I saw cops taking bribes, cops taking 'protection money' from drug dealers. I even saw a detective do somebody in and then load their body in the trunk of his car. I followed him and watched him later dump the woman's corpse down an abandoned mine shaft. His name was Herman Hobbs and he was out to get me. I made it my mission to expose him, but he blocked me every time. Worse yet, he tried to kill me. Thankfully, I was too fast for him.

"Then he started plotting to frame me, but I guess I really bought that on myself, big time. You see, after Leandra died, I took up with another chick that I met in class. Her name was Liluye Strömson and she was Apache right to the back bone. She was married to this Swedish fellow named Greg Strömson, so my affair with her was wrong. But I hooked up with her because I was still on the rebound from Leandra and she shared my interest in rocks and antique bottles. What's more, 'Lil' was very unhappy with her husband because the only bottle he was interested in was a full Jack Daniel's and he beat up on her whenever he got drunk, which was often, way too often.

"Besides taking all the same classes, Lil and I lived in the same Singing Saguaro Trailer Court just outside of Silver City which made it easy for me and her to see each other. This proximity also made it a sure thing that her husband would soon find us out. Lordy, what was I thinking.

"Greg, and I almost don't blame him, started acting out his jealous resentment in malicious little ways, like slashing the tires on my Volkswagen and breaking a window of my trailer. Stuff like that. I complained to the police about it, but they did nothing. Seems Det. Hobbs had poisoned all their minds against me. More than once he'd threatened me with bodily harm, but that didn't matter to them either.

"Then came the evening of judgment day, November 8, 1979, which spelled the end of everything for both of us. It was 7:47 and I was busy writing a term paper for my English Class when I got a frantic phone call from Lil. She practically screamed that Greg was dead and that she needed me over at her trailer 'right away'. I gave her some calming words and then hurried over. As soon as I got in the door I rushed to the living room where I found Lil wringing her hands and sobbing. All around her the trailer was splattered with blood, while on the floor in a big blood puddle lay Greg Strömson who was absolutely riddled with bullets. I asked her what happened and she told me that a man had come in and shot him and then tried to shoot her but missed. I further asked her what the man looked like and she said she couldn't tell because he had on a knitted, dark-blue ski mask. God, though, the chick was so broken up she could barely speak. The city patrol was making their rounds, so I took my Smith and Wesson out of my shoulder holster which I always wore, I'm from Texas, you know, and fired a shot just to get their attention. I got their attention all right. As bad luck would have it, the police car was staffed that night by Det. Hobbs and Rodger Deming, a cop who hated me and whom I know for a fact was in league with the asshole Hobbs.

"Together they arrested me and threw me in jail. A month later, I was tried for murder. Even so, the judge who was a grandfatherly black fellow named "Sam Clayton" got my sentence commuted to manslaughter. He really wanted to get me off completely, but his hands were tied by so-called legal authorities higher up than him. And dear Lil did her best to defend me, but that ratty Prosecuting Attorney, Hal Alamos, tore her to bloody shreds, verbally speaking. After my trial, she went and married an Apache dude. I hope he treats her well.

"As for me, I got a year in the New Mexico State Pen. After my release, I had that bad accident, but worse than that, my felony conviction has followed me everywhere like a malignant blood hound, preventing me from putting my roots down anywhere for very long. But in 1995, I did try it again in Montana with Licia," said James, ending his somber account with lowered eyes.

"Good God, James! What a sad, tragic, and beautiful story! I say beautiful because you obviously loved those two girls very much and the way you handled that frame job shows how brave and honest you are. But did you say you were in the state pen for a year? That's how long I was in..." I choked, I couldn't go any further.

"In where, cute circus chick?" asked James cuddling me closer.

"The Yakima State Mental Hospital!" I blurted out sobbing.

Then I began my own account of shame.

"It all started for me in 1977 too, when I was still on a farm in the mountainous outskirts of Quesnel, British Columbia, Canada. I lived 30 miles away from that town, but halfway in between lived a family from Hungary. They had a restaurant and I had a boutique and craft shop nearby. Their place was called 'The Paprika House' and mine was called 'Polestar Boutique.' Their last name was Låszlo and they had fled to Canada during the blood and thunder of the 1956 Hungarian Revolution. Fascinating people.

"There were three boys in the family – Attila, Adrian, and Alec. Alec was the youngest and I started dating him. He was handsome, charming, and a great cook who shared my interest

in short story and poetry writing. So I quickly fell in love with
him. I thought he loved me back, but I turned out to be badly
mistaken. Even so, we continued to date more and more often.
Soon we were making love.

"At the end of four months, our winter of love as I like to call
it, he told me that because I did stupid things, was not a problem
solver, and could not carry my end of a relationship, from then
on there would be no more love making or even kissing. He
would remain my friend though, he coldly, smugly reassured
me. I have never taken rejection very well and his digrading
our relationship to hands-off platonic was a form of rejection.
It shattered me, so much so that I attempted suicide and was
locked up for it.

"I spent a year in the lunatic asylum in Yakima, Washington,
because my parents, who had me committed, felt that Canada
didn't have the right mental health treatment facilities.

"When I got out I found that I was marked by society for my
time in that place, sort of like your own experience in jail. Like
you, I had real trouble holding onto a job, but I did the best I
could and got by. I avoided even friendships with men. What's
more, my rejection by Alec left me with permanently impaired
mental health.

"Then in 2000, my darling mother died and daddy and I left
Canada to be with my brother, Alan, and his side of the family
in Goldendale, Washington. Everything went well. Then I met
Wayne Gresham. He was a dapper, humorous, handsome little
Irish fellow who knew how to reach and comfort me when I
was feeling the most down. We met because he happened to
be working at the same thrift store I was employed at called
'Second Time Around'. Wayne and I started dating. Soon, I
moved into his big tan house on North King Street and we were
making love. He was a veteran of the Korean War and therefore, much older than me, but that didn't matter. Whenever two

hearts are truly in accord, age is not important.

"With my new love and new home, my life seemed to be going in a happy direction that could only get happier. I joined the local Golden Art Gallery and sold my artwork and crafts there, while getting orders for more. I made clothes, dolls, and cards and sold them at the Saturday Market. Wayne and I raised Miniature Schnauzer dogs and I was working on a book about the area's bounty of wildflowers. It was full of my original poems and drawings.

"But as much as I loved him, there were some aspects of my relationship with Wayne that made me desperately unhappy. For one thing, he was frequently mean and crabby. Also, he was greedy and stingy to the point of being scroogelike. Worst of all, he wouldn't marry me legally and that really hurt me, hurt me all the way down to my soul. Still, I stayed with him because the love between us was very strong.

"Then the wind turbines came to Goldendale and who should blow in on their propellers but my old flame, Alec. He had hired on as one of the wind technicians, 'propeller kings', I liked to call them. When we met and started bringing up memories of the many happy times we'd shared together, he swept me off my feet like I was being picked up by one of those massive wind tower's rotating blades. Alec, who had remained handsomer than ever was in addition sweet, patient, and generous. All of the things that Wayne wasn't.

"So I started seeing him behind Wayne's back. This went on for years, then in early 2010 Wayne found out about my ongoing affair with the Canadian propeller king. He was heartbroken. He even burst into tears. I felt so guilty.

"The next day, I broke up with Alec. But I guess the damage had already been done. The day after my final break up with Alec happened to be Memorial Day. I went out to do some errands and came home later to find my darling Wayne lying dead on the bathroom floor. I felt that his learning about my cheating on him was what killed him that evening. But there may have been other factors. He was a heavy smoker with a heart condition and was getting on in years. I took care of Checkers but she died shortly after he did. I believe that the little doggie died of a broken heart.

"After Wayne and Checkers died my whole world fell apart. I bought Taffy and began touring with an amateur traveling performance team. She would do tricks while I played an accordion. My partners did different things. One man did magic tricks. Another two did gymnastics. One lady was a quite stylish and clever clown. But though we traveled all over the US we could never, even with our combined talents, earn enough money to do more than survive.

"That's what I was doing when you picked me and Taffy up that wintry day many months ago. I had left my troupe to go see my Aunt in Saskatchewan. She and Uncle Ernest love animals so I was going to leave my dear little Taffy with them before traveling on to my destination," I said, wrapping up my own exposition with a slight taint of foreboding.

"Your destination to where, Bonnie love?" James asked, his voice showing just how deeply moved he was.

"My final destination," I replied softly with a touch of sadness in my voice.

At that moment my lover looked at me with an expression that was first startled, then sweetened with empathy. He didn't need to ask me what I meant by "final destination." With his caring, penetrating mind he just knew.

"Well then, circus chick, I'm very glad that me and my little Festiva snagged you and your flying monkey in time to change your direction along with your mind," said James with a smile that was sweet and at the same time serious.

"I'm very glad that you did too," I answered as I looked fondly at the man whom I knew to be my hero and savior in more ways than one.

"If the world would've lost you, it would have lost someone very precious. I am romantically attracted to you because you are a very romantic and loving person, with a capacity for devotion that is tremendous."

"But I wasn't very devoted to Wayne, now was I? Look how I cheated on him."

"I believe he pushed you into it, with his crabby and money-grubbing ways. He just didn't understand or appreciate you. Neither did that whirly gig guy. But rest assured, Bonnie love, I do."

I replied to his kind words with a kiss. Then after putting Taffy to bed in her room, James and I made love on the divan in a way that was sweeter and more passionate than we ever had before. We had truly and completely bared our souls to each other. There is no greater aphrodisiac.

Chapter Seven

James and I decided to get out of Dickinson. We sold our
museum home, furnishings and all, then hit the road in our little
Festiva with a bewildered Taffy. Both of us knew what we had
to do. James needed to get an expungement, possibly a retrial.
Expungement meaning his felony record would be sealed or
destroyed so that it could no longer be used against him. While
I needed to pursue my dream of writing and illustrating a book
about wildflowers. Together, we would support each other in
our goals and trials.

But first of all my beefy companion and I wanted to clear our
heads with a whirlwind trip through the great American Southwest. We went from the Dakotas to Wyoming where we spent
a whole month taking in the wonders of Yellowstone National
Park, lofty feldspar Devil's Tower, which is actually the plug of
an extinct volcano, and Fossil Butte National Monument. That
latter site lived up to its name and thrilled us with its wealth
of Eocene Era lake sediment fossils of fish, reptiles, birds,
mammals, insects, and plants. When the hike of the day was
done, James and I would pitch our tent at Pike's Peak or Bridg-
er-Teton National Forest. One night we even braved camping at
Hell's Half Acre with its rocky bare valleys and towering jagged
peaks and pillars. After making love, we talked for hours about
basaltic lava fields, of which that rugged geologic site is one
outstanding example. After getting permission from the park's
authorities, James and I spent a day at mountain-flanked Grand

Teton National Park digging out a pioneer privy site. We found a few medicine bottles and better yet, a cameo and an intact Shoshone Indian bead necklace, all of which we were permitted to keep. We had Taffy carry away dirt in a little bucket all the time we were excavating.

"Do you know how these mountains were named 'The Grand Tetons', cute guy," I asked as I paused in my own shoveling to gaze up at the group of three gnarly mountains behind me.

"Yes, circus chick. Some French explorer thought they looked like tits, so he called them Les Trois Tétons, or The Three Tits," explained James with a mischievous wink as he dusted off his latest find, a clear glass cough syrup bottle, probably dating from 1881.

"Ha ha. Thanks for the mammaries!"

"Damn right!"

After spending a whole month taking in everything that Wyoming could offer, the three of us were on our way to Utah. June had turned into July.

From the corner of Wyoming that jutted into "The Beehive State," James and I made a beeline into a land of breathtaking contrasts. From desiccated hills and massive sandstone arches and pillars, we traveled through small homey towns with 19 [th] Century brick buildings. One of these was Moab where we ate breakfast at the Love Muffin Cafe and yes, the place lived up to its name. The muffins there were excellent. The restaurant owner wouldn't let us bring Taffy in with us, so we bought a banana muffin just for her. Next we toured the cities including majestic Salt Lake City with its clean streets and towering skyscrapers. All three of us waved at the golden statue of the Angel Moroni as we drove past the Mormon Bountiful Temple.

On July 4 th, James, Taffy, and I spent the whole day at This Is The Place Heritage Park, which lies just outside of the Utah State Capitol. It was a searing hot day, nearly 100 °, but we were up to it. We put on extra sunscreen and western hats with wide brims. We bought a little pink plaid poke bonnet for Taffy. Then happy as bees in a flower patch, we rode all three of the replica steam engines that chugged through the park and afterwards looked over its restored 19th Century Homestead.

"You know how this place got its name, circus chick?" James asked as we strolled into the booth lined section of the park where food and souvenirs were sold.

"No, cute guy, how did it get that name?" I asked as I took in the vast variety of concession stands.

"From Brigham Young himself. When he and his flock first arrived in this area, he looked all around and then told them that 'This is the place'."

"Ha ha. That was kind of an off the wall way of telling 'em they'd just found paradise on earth."

"Well, old Brigham Young was an off the wall kind of guy sometimes."

"Yeah. I heard he was too."

Finally, we settled on a booth that sold watermelon slices and was run by a family dressed in authentic looking pioneer clothes. It was late afternoon and we three were hankering for a cool treat to tide us over until supper. James paid for the watermelon slices and we enjoyed them on a tree-shaded picnic table.

When our juicy fruit snack was done, we resumed our tour of the old buildings. Time passed quickly and then we returned to our picnic table for our evening meal. Later on, we were treated to a grand fireworks display. It was still hot that evening, so my hefty companion and I ordered a pitcher of lemonade from the watermelon vendors, spread a blanket on the grass, and spent the rest of the night watching the thrilling panorama of colored pinwheels and showers of light in the deepening sky. Taffy looked up at the bright display and chattered with joy.

We didn't forget the ghost towns of which Utah has an impressive number and variety. One of these, Eureka, had been a busy mining town in 1870. Utah has a Silver City too, albeit one that has gone to wreck and ruin since 1930. While passing through it, we took photos of ourselves posing with Taffy by the remains of the Knight silver and gold smelter there.

During the last few days of July, James, Taffy, and I visited the Cleveland-Lloyd Dinosaur Quarry and several other fossil rich sites. We also went to the Navajo Indian Reservation in San Juan County where a man who owned a trading post honored us by making a sand painting for our good luck and edification. It was all done in red, gold, and black and full of zigzags, lines, triangles, and swastikas.

"They all show you three are on a special journey of redemption which will result in better fortune and love," explained the trading post fellow whose name was Ahiga and who was also an accomplished silver smith.

Because he liked jewelry and because Ahiga had made a sand painting especially for us, James bought three silver and turquoise pieces from the thoughtful "smithy" and trader. These were a silver ring with a turquoise setting in the shape of a grasshopper for himself, a bow-shaped silver barrette with a turquoise heart setting for Taffy, and a silver necklace with a turquoise honey bee pendant for me.

But my brawny boyfriend didn't give it to me right then. He waited until we were camped for the night at the Butch Cassidy

Campgrounds just outside of the town of Salina.

"For you, Bonnie love, because you are as industrious as a little bee and as sweet as honey. And you're more than just any bee, you're my Queen Bee," said James softly as he fastened the bee pendant necklace around my neck and kissed my nape.

We were in our tent with our bed roll waiting for us. Taffy was bedded down in her own little sleeping bag beside of James' boots. I walked over to a mirror that I'd pinned on one of the tent's sides so I could take a better look at the lively gift I'd just been given.

"James, it's beautiful and I will do my best to live up to the virtues this little insect represents," I said and then thanked him with a kiss on the mouth.

He returned my kiss with equal passion and then with the moist heat of the evening all around us, we made sweet love on our camp bed roll.

The next day, James and I packed up our things and headed out of the beehive that is the State of Utah. We and our monkey had eaten our fill of the honey it had to offer in the way of amusements and so it was time for us to be back on the road again. July had now turned to August and we were headed for Arizona.

It was hot traveling in the American Southwest during the full heat of summer, but we were equipped to weather it. Our little car had a good air conditioning system and we made sure there was always cool water on hand for us to drink and splash our faces with. Then too, we often rode the highways by night and bedded down for camping siestas in the daytime.

Our threesome traveling party furthermore dodged the searing heat by keeping to the Northern Plateau Region of the state. We especially toured and photographed the natural wonders at and near Flagstaff, Sedona, and Winslow. These included the 37 mile wide Barringer Meteor Crater, tall ruddy sandstone Cathedral rock, and of course, the steep and rugged peaks of the famous Grand Canyon. More than once, we visited the 70 foot Indian Watchtower. This circular masonry edifice rises from a rubble base and is painted on the inside with ancient Pueblo word pictures.

One dry pleasant day we were standing in the shadow of this lofty, gray, window-crowned tower and noticed a cloud of grasshoppers stirring in the dun-colored dust near our feet. Suddenly, the peace of their wing flicking and raspy buzzing was broken when a Pueblo Indian fellow in blue jeans, a blue shirt, and carrying a boom box on his shoulder came up the rocky, aspen and honey mesquite shaded escarpment behind the soaring tower. He was about our age. We smiled at him and he smiled back as he kept on walking. Just then, the dozen for so grasshoppers took wing and flew off.

The man disappeared into a grove of blue spruce, however the song from his portable sound system continued to drift over to us and flood us with memories. It was an old favorite I hadn't heard in a while – The Eagles' hypnotically, smooth-rockin' tune "Witchy Woman." Evidently, this song was one of James' favorites too because he began to whistle along to it. Not to be outdone, I joined him on my little accordion. Then he left off whistling and pulled out his harmonica. Taffy also lent her small jabbering voice to the whole impromptu songfest. Soon, a small knot of people had collected around us, smiling and clapping their hands to the beat.

"Woo hoo witchy woman,
She got the moon in her eye."

Before many more lines were sung, the song had faded into the aerie of dry mountain air while our audience vanished into the rocky desert scenery, leaving my bull necked lover and me alone with the silence of many unanswered questions. Even Taffy had grown quiet as she squatted down in the dust picking up and examining some stones from a pile in front of her as though she in her own monkey way was looking for answers to questions too. James slipped his harmonica back in his jeans pocket and turned to me with an impish grin.

"Funny how that song always reminds me of my ex," he commented as the red of a desert sunset began to creep across the late noon sky.

"By your 'ex' you really mean Lícia, don't you," I replied somewhat petulantly while feeling the green monster spring to life in my belly. Her divorcing James to marry his motorcycle stuntman brother was a scandal that had made big news in every tabloid in American.

"Yes, who else could I mean?"

"Do-do you still love her? If she divorced your brother or if he died during one of his stunts and left her a widow, would you remarry her?"

"After everything she did to hurt me, hell no on all three counts. But I am still fond of her and always will be. Please respect and try to understand that, Bonnie. However, remarrying Lícia would be like marrying the Devil. I've gotten to the point where I can honestly say that my psychopath brother can have her. They deserve each other."

"It's quite all right, James. I completely understand," I said, than I felt the ache of something still being stuck in my emotional craw.

"If "Witchy Woman" always reminds you of Lícia, are there any songs that remind you of me?" I asked my voice grating slightly with an edge of peevishness.

"Why yes, Bonnie love," said James suddenly and brightly, "Best Of My Love" and "I Love To Watch A Woman Dance" by the same Eagles rock group never fail make me think fond loving thoughts of you. But on your dark side, and everyone has a dark side, you make me think of "99 Red Balloons" by Nena. While Lícia could be a witch when she was out to get somebody, you can be a weapon of mass destruction whenever you're angry."

"Ha ha. Thank you, cute guy, I didn't know I had that kind of power."

"You have a lot more power than you think, sweet cheeks."

I felt much relieved then and also amused by James' inimitable words and feelings. Satisfied, I deftly changed the tract of speech to something more uplifting for both of us.

"That song 'Witchy Woman' by The Eagles always reminds me of somebody too, a fictional character I was writing about when it first made the Top Ten," I said, my sense of growing relief calming me so I could recall past literary projects.

"Oh, what sort of fictional character were you writing about then, circus chick?" asked James with a fellow writer's interest.

"Her name was Allanana and she was, in my personal mythology, an ancient Queen of Libya. She ruled with an iron fist, but she could also be very kind and just when the situation called for it. But along with having tremendous political and military power, she was also a very powerful sorceress.

"Fascinating! Your Allanana sounds a lot like the magical warrior Queen Circe of classical Greek Mythology. It's good to base your characters on the ancient mythos. I do that a lot."

"Circe was sort of who I had in mind when I dreamed up my

Allanana. However, she was different from her in one respect, as gifted as she was in the magical arts, she never turned any men into animals."

"There's more than one way a woman can turn a man into an animal, cute circus girl."

"Giggle. How very true."

At that moment, Taffy began some lively chittering as if to say, men or male animals, there's not a lot of difference.

Both of us laughed.

With Taffy in tow, James and I spent the rest of the day exploring the inside of the Grand Canyon's majestic tower and the jagged high mountain plateaus surrounding it. When the setting sun began to blaze flames of red and orange across the gray-blue desert sky we stood and admired it for awhile. Then we found a spot for our tent at the landmark's Grand Canyon Railway RV Park and after tucking Taffy in spent the night into the red inflamed first breaking of dawn conjuring up poems and stories centered around Allanana, my mythical warrior Queen, and the antics of grasshoppers.

In the final version of the epic Queen's story, we portrayed her as a Hopi Indian chieftainess whose name was Tablita and who used grasshoppers as messengers, much like the Norse God Odin used crows.

We spent the next day riding one of the recreation park's restored steam locomotives which took us from the Old West-style town of Williams to The Grand Canyon's South Rim. Taffy's large brown eyes grew wide with wonder as our train steamed up into pine-studded, arid hills and steeply down into rocky dusty valleys.

When day turned to late afternoon, my husky lover, my monkey, and I braved the 106° above temperatures and rode to Phoenix where we had a picnic supper at a local park and then enjoyed a late night ballet being featured at historic Orpheum Theatre. The ballet being featured that night was a presentation in dance form of the ancient Greek myth of Prometheus, the Titan who first brought the gift of fire to humanity. The dancers leaped, promenaded, and pirouetted to the fervent notes of Beethoven's "Creatures of Prometheus" Opus 43, the ballet the one being presented that night was loosely based on. What's more, the choreographer had intertwined the legendary Phoenix Bird, that dies in fire and then is reborn from the ashes, as part of the stage decor. So an enormous, flat, stained glass phoenix towered and glistened above the performers as they danced the tale of one man's defiance of the gods and subsequent fall from grace.

In one especially spectacular scene in the ballet which was actually titled "Prometheus", the hero dressed in red and carrying a prop torch leaped and spun under the glass phoenix. As he capered, six men and six women dressed in either yellow or orange to represent licking flames, danced around him. The dance extravaganza being played out there in the splendor of that Spanish Baroque theater with its intricate murals and moldings was entrancing and almost hypnotic – like staring at a real flickering candle flame can be. So engrossed were James and I that we barely noticed someone sitting down beside us in the third front row where we were watching from. It was none other than our famous friend, Addy.

"Hello strangers," he said in a low voice. "How's it been?"

"The shits. Both of us got canned," answered James as he turned to give the thin man a pained smile.

"We've been traveling the Southwest to get our minds off it," I chimed in as I bounced Taffy on my lap.

She jabbered a "Hello!" at him as she reached for him with both of her front paws. Addy fondly patted her on the head. I noticed that he was garbed all in white as was typical of him. Looking his summery best, the stunt biker had on short white boots, white jeans, and a white T-shirt with a picture of a beautiful motorcycle riding angel on it.

"I'm very sorry to hear that, guys. But trust me, things will get better," he said as he fixed us with an icy blue stare which had an element of unexpected warmth.

"How can you be sure of that? How can you say that?" James asked in a tone of playful sarcasm.

"Believe me, dude, I just know," answered Addy in a way that smoothly dodged James verbal thrusts.

"We haven't seen you in a long while. How have things been with you, Addy?" I interjected while dividing my attention between the dancers in red, orange, and yellow and our mysterious friend in cloudy white.

"I won two motocross races, both in California, since I saw you last. Also, I did a 200 foot stunt jump over a line of monster trucks at Nevada's Sam Boyd Stadium," revealed Addy who was himself getting caught up in the spirited dance on the stage before us.

"I know all about those races in Milestone and Pauma Valley and how you won them. I even wrote articles about them for my newspaper. I was so proud of you," said James brightening up.

"We saw both races while we were still in Dickinson and heard a live radio broadcast about your Sam Boyd stunt while we were going though Utah. That was exciting," I commented as I remembered the excitement I felt while listening to the well-publicized sports event.

"I'm glad I gave you guys some thrills. It's what I love doing best," as our main man said this, Taffy crawled over into his lap.

"I guess now, my friend, you'll be mostly gearing up for the event in October," ventured James as the music onstage began to reach a crescendo and the dancers moved around with more vigor.

"Yes, October," replied Addy with a smile as he handed Taffy back to me.

"I liked the way you announced on live TV that your death had been all staged as a publicity stunt and as a dig at Maximilian," as I said this, I turned my gaze from the climactic scene on stage to our friend in white.

But he was gone! In his place was a wad of $100 bills. Just then, the ballet came to a dramatic end with trumpets blaring and cymbals crashing while a dozen dancers in white robes who represented irate gods carried Prometheus over to a huge onstage boulder and chained him to it as punishment for purloining their fire as a gift to humanity. While the red stage curtain came down and the ballet troupe took their bows to a thunderous burst of clapping, James slipped the money into his chained wallet.

"Dear Addy always knows when we need him the most, doesn't he, cute circus chick?" James commented as he looked at me with a sly grin.

"Yes, he sure does, cute guy," I said feeling tired, but fulfilled.

We joined in the clapping and then walked out from the oasis of the theater's air conditioned coolness into the parched heat of night. Because it was still 106° at that after midnight hour and therefore too hot for us to bed down at a campground, we checked in at the downtown Phoenix Sunrise Motel.

That last night of August in the cool embrace of the motel room and the loving security of my sweetheart's arms, I drifted into a very strange and portentous dream. Taffy had dozed off on a blanket on the thick carpet nearby. In this nocturnal journey I heard a chorus of chirping grasshoppers, while two of these very same insects, a large black one and a red one of equal size, fought each other fiercely.

Chapter Eight

James, Taffy, and I woke up very early the next morning. It was so early that the blazing sun wasn't even up and the stars in the cool desert sky were just starting to blink out. We traveled farther across the arid land. When we came to the town of Tombstone, James drove into a roadside park with adobe outhouses and sidewalks lined with tall yucca plants.

"We will have breakfast here, Bonnie love," announced my sturdy boyfriend as he parked near a picnic site that had a worn wooden table and a camp fire pit ringed with stones.

"Looks like a good spot, cute guy," I agreed as I grabbed my still-drowsy monkey and left the car with her. After all three of us had made use of the picnic ground's pit toilets, James and I got busy preparing breakfast.

All three of us were already very hungry. To help her last until the meal was ready I gave Taffy a banana and some milk in a sippy cup.

As the olive tones of dawn's first glow began to lighten the dusty horizon, James brought out our portable gas cook stove and pumped it into life. With a hiss and a puff, tongues of blue light began to lick up from the burners. On that cue, I put bacon grease in a pan and quickly rolled some shredded beef and vegetables into breakfast burritos which I laid in the sizzling grease.

In between tending the burritos, I filled our coffee pot with water and coffee and set it to brewing. While I put myself to these tasks, James held Taffy on his lap and told me some interesting stories of adventures he had years ago in Tombstone.

"I lived there in 1987," he began. "And I knew this Navaho fellow who was a rug weaver and a shaman. He claimed that the end of the world was coming soon and often weaved apocalyptic messages into the designs of his rugs. And the old fellow wasn't too far off, 'cause it is the end of the world, sweet cheeks."

"How interesting. Kind of reminds me of one of my favorite songs, James honey," I retorted with a touch of mischief in my voice.

"And what song might that be?"

"'It's The End Of The World As We Know It (And I Feel Fine)' by REM," as I dished up the burritos, I then launched into singing that fast-paced, almost mock-End Times 1987 hit rock tune. James smiled.

"It's not one of my favorite songs. All the same, I like it better than 'Eve Of Destruction' by Barry Mcguire. God, that was morbid," commented James with a laugh.

"I think it was a morbid song too and I never cared for it," I said as I poured his and my coffee. Then I sat down beside him and took Taffy in my arms. James prayed over our food and then he turned to me.

"I've been thinking and I've decided that one of the many things that makes you a far better companion for me than Lícia ever was is that no matter what I say, you always respond with a sense of humor that's adorable. Like the way you answered my comment about it being the end of the world by singing that crazy song. Not at all like Lícia would have answered," com-

66

mented James as he took a mouthful of his burrito. I had made two for him, one for myself, and a half of one for Taffy.

"And what would her reply have been, muscle guy?" I asked as I followed my bite of burrito with a sip of coffee.

"She would have said in a whiny voice that I should learn to think more positively."

"The girl sounds like she could be a real whiner."

"She could be when she felt like it."

As the three of us worked on our breakfast, the rising sun began to bathe our surroundings in the scarlet of dawn and we changed our topic of discussion back to the apocalyptic rug weaver.

"His name was Sani Joe and he claimed he could make some of his rugs fly..." continued James as I poured him another cup of coffee.

He finished his story, while me and Taffy finished our breakfast. Afterwards, James packed the stove back into the Festiva's trunk, while I did the dishes. Under a climbing desert sun, we all got into the vehicle and we were on the road heading out of Tombstone, with the music of one of his Eagles albums to guide us on our way. With our stomach's full, we felt happy and content.

But, when we were only a mile from the campground, James started to wince and rub his eyes.

"What's wrong, cute guy?" I asked in alarm as he temporarily lost control of the car and then pulled it over to the shoulder of the road. After parking, he put his handkerchief to his eyes and hunched over.

"It's my eyes! They're stinging like the devil and I can barely see!" he replied with a moan.

"Here, James love, let me help," I said as I took his red hand-kerchief and put some cool water on it from my water jug.

Then I bathed his eyes with it. That seemed to help, but as I nursed his stricken eyes, I noticed that they were blood shot and there was mucus oozing from their corners.

"We need to get you to a doctor," I said evenly.

James agreed and told me where the hospital in Tombstone was located. As he continued to bury his burning eyes in the wet handkerchief, I took his place in the driver's seat and we were on our way back into Tombstone.

I am not the best driver in the world. In fact, I have always disliked driving, however, a person can amaze themselves when they are called upon by a loved one in need to do something they don't usually do. With the Festiva's steering wheel in my hands, I got my boyfriend to the emergency ward of The Tombstone Family Health Clinic. Leaving Taffy in the car with a cookie and some reassuring words, I then helped James find his way to the emergency ward's entrance where he checked in.

After he signed a few papers, we waited. In a short while, he was seen by a doctor who examined his eyes very thoroughly. I stayed with him sitting in the background the whole while.

"That's quite a bad infection you got there, young fellow," said the general practitioner who was a tall balding fellow named Dr. Crane.

"I know, sir, it feels like the sand man dumped too much in my eyeballs last night," remarked James as the doctor set aside the light he had been using to explore my boyfriend's stricken orbs.

"Not sand, James. More like a bug. You have a type of staph infection. Here, I'm going to ease it with some antibiotic drops," continued Dr. Crane as he opened each of James' eyes wider and put one drop in each from a small plastic bottle.

"It's like a sleepy bug infestation," I said trying to ease the situation with a little humor.

"Sleepy bugs" were what my mother always called those small crusts that form in everyone's eyes overnight. She wasn't too far off in calling them that since scientists have discovered that we all have tiny microbe "bugs" all over on our skin. Thinking of them began to make me feel somewhat crawly, so I pushed thoughts of the creepy, little creatures away and returned my thoughts to James and what he was going through at the moment. After gently inserting the eye drops, Dr. Crane gave him the whole bottle and wrote up a prescription for a another bottle. He then dismissed him with the suggestion that he go pay a visit to a local ophthalmologist.

"Because there's something besides that staph infection I feel you should check out," he said in a serious tone.

"Like what, sir?" asked James as he quickly pocketed the eye drops.

"Like a possible cataract, James," said Dr. Crane as he handed h im a referral to the Southwestern Eye Center in Sierra Vista. "Go see Dr. Torrance there, he's the best cataract specialist around."

James promised to check him out. That same day, he made an appointment to see Dr. Torrance and we spent the rest of the day looking over Tombstone. With Taffy in hand, we went to the OK Corral and witnessed a reenactment of the famous gun fight with the Erp brothers and Doc Holiday on one side and the Clanton "Cowboys" on the other.

"I once wrote a story connected with the event, James," I said to my lover after the gun smoke had cleared and the actors portraying Wyatt and the rest had taken their bows.

"Did you really, sweet cheeks? And what was your twist on this wild west showdown? Knowing you, I bet it was original,"remarked my sturdy lover.

"It was, cute guy. I had a character based on me as Doc Holiday's gambling sweet heart, Big Nose Kate and I had Wayne as Doc Holiday. He would have made a great Doc Holiday. I focused more on the exciting ups and downs of their romance than on the gunfight. And I still have a copy of it somewhere," I explained as the sun above us steadily climbed over the steel fence and gun powder fine sand that formed an outdoor stage for the feigned, but historically accurate gun fight and the crowd begin to disperse.

"And did you see me too in that splendid reenactment?" asked James in a tone that hinted that now he was feeling the gnawing of jealousy.

"Yes, James love. You would be the best Wyatt Erp ever," I reassured him.

He sealed that reassurance with a kiss and then we gathered up Taffy and headed for Big Nose Kate's saloon where we enjoyed a beer with steak and potatoes. Our monkey had a potato while basking in the attention of the waitresses, who were dressed like real wild west dance hall girls – all ruffles and low necklines.

"You need to get a dress like that, Bonnie love, you'd look gorgeous dressed like that," said James with a saucy wink.

"You think I could find one for sale in this town?" I asked, delighted by his sweet compliment.

"I'm positive," said James as he downed his beer and then prepared to order another one.

After our meal we took in the beauty of the nearby Bird Cage Theater with its authentic 19ᵗʰ Century décor. This included lavish murals and a fully equipped poker room.

"They say this place is haunted," remarked James in a whisper.

"I've heard that too. How about us coming back here tonight and checking it out for ghosts?" I suggested mischievously.

"Or better yet, Bonnie love. We could spend the night here."

"Do you think they'd let us, cute guy?"

"They wouldn't need too. I'm an old hand at sneaking into places and hiding out."

"Then let's do it, you rascal. Whether we see a ghost or not, being in that old place after hours might supply us with inspiration for writing a book."

"Ha ha. I like your spirit, circus chick."

With the exciting expectation of spending the night at the purportedly ghost-ridden old entertainment emporium, James, Taffy, and I spent the rest of the day touring the other legendary buildings that Tombstone had to offer. We strolled through Schlieffelin Hall and had supper at Crystal Palace Saloon.

We also found a Navajo Cultural Museum on the outskirts of the city that featured an impressive display of woven baskets. Looking at their designs in tan and sandy yellow made me recall my own attempts at basket weaving, which were far less impressive but still loads of fun. To add to the enjoyment of the tour, we found a man who was on the site weaving authentic Navajo baskets who was happy to demonstrate and explain his skill in detail.

After looking over the basket exhibits, James drove Taffy and me to see some of Tombstone's more out of the way spots of interest. One of them was the Ed Schieffelin Monument. This tall sandstone cairn with a base which narrowed to a smooth top is actually the grave maker of Mr. Schieffelin, the founder of the historic mining town. Tombstone had been built on his discoveries as a prospector for silver. The three of us were the only ones there by his cairn at the time.

"This reminds me of a cenotaph I saw once while I was living in Canada. It was a memorial to local men who had served in World War I and it was about this size and shape. That monument was built of granite instead of sandstone, but the resemblance is uncanny," I remarked as I looked up and down the stone structure's rugged sides.

"They are similar because they're both stone grave markers and, according to you, both are sort of cone shaped. The dissimilarity in rock material is revealing, however. Sandstone is common to Arizona, while British Columbia has several granite mines," said James with fascinatingly adroitness.

"That's my James, ever the mineralogist," I retorted with a laugh that I followed with a butterfly quick kiss on his cheek.

As we were discussing the weathered grave stone, Taffy had been sitting at its base playing with a pile of loose sandstone rocks. Then to our delight, we watched her start piling them into a simple dolmen. That is, a pile of upright stones with one stone balanced on top for a "roof".

"Why Taffy," exclaimed James with delight as he bent closer to look over her creation. "You're quite the builder! Did you teach her how to do this, Bonnie love, or did she just pick it up on her own?

"I must have, cute guy. But I've never seen her do this before with rocks, always wooden blocks. Also, she still isn't able to form words with them. Even so, she's very good at stacking things so they balance," I said proudly as I crouched down in the dust near her and patted her furry head. She looked up and chattered at both of us affectionately.

"Ha ha. What a clever little monkey! But we better get her out of here before she starts building her own version of Stonehenge." said James as he gently lifted both of us to our feet.

"That would really be something to write a book about. Have you ever been to Stonehenge, James?" I asked, assuming that he may have since he was so well traveled.

"No I haven't. Actually, I've never been to the British Isles."

"I've been to Stonehenge, James, honey."

"You have? When, circus doll? Tell me all about it."

"Ha ha. Not the original Stonehenge, but there's a perfect replica of it outside of Goldendale where I used to live. Looks like the real thing too and it's a place where druids and wiccan types from all over come and do their rituals every winter and spring solstice."

"Do they sacrifice animals there or just virgins."

"Ha ha. No, but they do burn a lot of smudge sticks and do a lot of chanting. They also wear long robes. Some of them wear deer antlers."

"Then you've seen them do their thing, circus chick."

"More than once, James."

"You will have to take me to one of their pagan gatherings, Bonnie love. Someday, when we happen to be in the area."

"It's a plan, but you'll have to wear a dark robe."

"I will if you sew one for me, sweet cheeks."

"I can do that, cute guy. They're very simple to make."

From the wind-worn prospector's grave marker, we drove to the site of his mining tunnels, which he named The Good Enough Mine. This site featured regular tours down its shaft's 70 foot underground expanse with a guide who was talkative and friendly. This guide, was a young man named "Pete" who dressed like a prospector of the time when the mine was first opened. He led us with five other people down into its deepest reaches which were well-lit the whole way.

"This system of mining tunnels, folks, leads directly under the entire length of the city of Tombstone," he explained as we followed him through the passages that had ceilings buttressed by heavy wooden supports.

Along the way, he directed our attention to the copper ore deposits that could still be found in the mine shaft's walls. They were a beautiful peacock greenish blue and seemed to be oozing from the sandstone surrounding us.

"This was set up as a silver mine," our guide revealed. "But copper, gold, and lead were also found down here."

Now and then, Pete directed our attention to the various pieces of mining equipment and the heavy ore wagons that could be seen in nearly every section of the mine.

"Sure reminds me of my own mining days, when I moiled for lead and zinc in Utah. Only my tools were a lot less primitive," remarked James as we stopped to inspect an ore bucket. It was huge enough to carry a man and ton of unrefined silver.

I nodded and grinned in agreement as I hoisted Taffy higher on my shoulders and followed my lover as our guide led us down, down to the mine's egress. Soon, we were all back out in the blazing sun and after our eyes adjusted to the bright light of day, we got back in the Ford Festiva and continued our tour. Of course, we spent a long time looking over the Boothill Grave-yard and taking photos. Towards the end of our jaunt we went to a 1880s theme dress shop were I bought my dance hall girl dress. It was low cut in front, had plenty of ruffles, and was as greenish blue as the copper deposits in the mine where we'd just visited. I wore the gown for the rest of our time in Tombstone. Wearing it made me feel as light and lovely as the desert breeze. James was obviously delighted by it.

"Wow, Bonnie, sweet cheeks. That dress makes you look sexier than a saloon wall painting," he said as he looked me up and down with a grin.

"Thank you, my handsome cowboy," I said as I returned his compliment with a kiss.

"Looking as gorgeous as you do in that dress, I have to take you to eat at the Longhorn Restaurant," invited James as he offered me his sturdy arm. By then it was suppertime and all three of us were famished from our wanderings around Tombstone.

"I would be delighted, James love," I said as I wrapped my own arm around his.

Beside us Taffy was walking and chattering quite excitedly. All of the places and people she had seen that day had really given her a thrill, especially since I had gotten her a pretty yellow bonnet at the same store where I had bought my dress.

"You're my cute little monkey, yes you are," said James as he bent over to pull the front of her bonnet down teasingly over her tiny face. In response, she gave the monkey equivalent of a giggle.

At the Longhorn we had a late supper and then crept stealthily into the Bird Cage Theater where we spent the night in a corner of the Poker Room, undetected. I swear that James could break in anywhere if he put his mind to it. But though the zombie gambler manikin who happened to be standing at one of the room's card-strewn tables was creepy enough, he didn't bother us trespassers as we went to sleep all cuddled up together. We didn't see or hear any ghosts either, even though the moaning of the desert wind outside seemed to carry the whispers of theater guests a long time gone. Our luck held up and when morning came James, Taffy, and I were able to get out of the old theater the way we had gotten in without being caught. This was because James knew about a secret trap door, once used by outlaws, that lead from the song hall's basement to The Good Enough Mine's own system of tunnels.

That morning, we had breakfast at the Longhorn and then boarded the Festiva for the 18 mile trip to James' appointment with the eye specialist in Sierra Vista. On the way, we enjoyed a bounty of beautiful scenery. On both sides of the road were craggy mountains and low plains verdant with bushes and tall yucca plants.

By 2:00 pm, we reached Sierra Vista on time for James' eye examination by Dr. Torrance. I sat with Taffy in the waiting room as he approached the girl at the admissions desk. She was a lovely Hispanic with a pronounced accent.

"Hola, Señor Schönhausse. Just have a seat and the Doctor

weel be weeth you soon," she said as she gave him some papers to sign and a pen.

"Gracias," he replied as he took the medical info and registration papers and joined the seat beside me and Taffy who was playing with a fake pair of sunglasses.

After making out the documents that mostly asked questions about his medical history, my lover returned them to the little receptionist and then plopped back down in his seat. He patted Taffy on the head and then became engrossed in reading a *Time* magazine article about North Korean leader Kim Jong-Un and his rising career as a threat to the rest of the world, while I looked over the latest make-up and fashion trends in an *Allure* glamour magazine.

Very soon a thin ophthalmic nurse with blonde hair and glasses appeared from a door.

"James, the doctor will see you now," she said pleasantly, but matter-of-factly.

"I'm here," said my burly boyfriend as he left his seat and put down his magazine on a small wooden table with the others. "You can come too, Bonnie."

Without needing a second invite, I put away my own magazine and gathered up Taffy, all set to follow James into the examination room. The nurse, however, objected to Taffy being part of the party.

"Sorry, miss, no pets allowed. You can't bring your monkey in here," she informed me.

"Okay," I said, "I understand."

On that cue, I reluctantly returned with Taffy to the Festiva.

But before I left, the receptionist salved my feelings and Taffy's by giving her a banana flavored lolly pop and a smile.

I put Taffy in the car and turned on the air conditioner since it was blistering hot out.

"Now you be a good girl, Taffy. We'll be right back soon," I reassured her as I handed her the lolly pop and followed that with a kiss on her furry cheek. She thanked me with soft cooing sounds.

A moment later, I was back in the coolness of the ophthalmologist's clinic. I asked the receptionist the way to the room where James was being examined, explaining to her that I was his girlfriend. With a broad smile, she led me to the room herself.

"Gracias, miss," I told her with a nod.

"De nada (You're welcome) and you have such a cute monkey," she replied as I walked in the room to find James seated in a chair getting ready for a whole series of tests. Both he and the doctor favored me with smiles of greeting.

"Come in Miss Bonnie and have a seat. You must be James' significant other. He's been saying all kinds of good things about you," invited the eye doctor as he kindly directed me to a seat over in the corner, where I would be out of the way, but still able to view my lover as he was put through the battery of tests.

"Thanks, Doctor, I do my best," I replied with a laugh as I took my seat.

At that moment, the eye specialist directed James' attention to a chart directly in front of him on the wall. This chart contained letters of graduated size and was meant to test my cute guy's visual acuity or sharpness and clarity of vision. Dr. Torrance had him look at the letters while wearing his glasses and without his glasses. When the doctor was satisfied, he took him through several more tests. Some being very technical while others being surprisingly simple. In the confrontational field test, James was directed to cover one eye with a black paddle while his examiner waved his hand in front of him. Both of his eyes were tested this way. This was followed by some extraocular movement or eye muscle tests and involved James covering each eye in turn with the same plastic paddle. The doctor waved a pen in front of him in all directions, while telling him to keep his free eye "glued" to it.

"Ha ha. But I never let glue get in my eyes," Joked James as he forced himself to keep his attention on the roving pen. "I have seen people get that Crazy Glue stuff in their eyes though. Their eyelids would be sealed shut for days afterward.

"Good for you, James. I've had to treat people who did that to themselves. Lucky for them, there was no permanent damage done and a little medical salve always got them unstuck. Almost always, that taught them a lesson to think before they rubbed their eyes while working with the stuff and I never saw them again with that problem," said Dr. Torrance with a smile as all three of us had a good laugh while he prepared to continue with the rest of the tests.

Next, James' eye pupils were tested three ways. First came the light response pupil test. This gauged how his pupils changed size in response to light. The Ophthalmologist dimmed the lights in the room and then had my lover fix his gaze on the potted cactus that stood on a nearby shelf. While he stared at the small prickly plant, Dr. Torrance shone a small pocket light in first his right eye, then his left. Secondly, came the swinging flashlight pupil test which compared each of his pupil's reactions to light. Dr. Torrance dimmed the room's lights again and then swung his pen light before my boyfriend who had his eyes focused on the tiny globular barrel cactus in the earthen ware container. This was to find if both his pupils contracted or dilated the same.

For the third and final near response pupil test, the eye doctor turned all of the lights on and had James pin his eyes on the cactus again while he waved a blank card in front of him. This was to assess how quickly James' pupils constricted as his focus changed from far to near.

At that juncture, I left and went to look after Taffy. I found her sound asleep with the lolly pop handle stuck in her hair. I gently removed it, took her potty in a nearby park, and then put her back in the car with a glass of cool water. I also kept the air conditioner going. Both the water and air conditioner were necessities since it was 106° outside.

When I returned to the exam room, I found Dr. Torrance putting James through a cover test. This was done to measure how well his eyes worked together. This exam was the simplest one so far. The Ophthalmologist had James stare at the cactus again as he covered each eye and then uncovered it. He did this to gauge each of his eyes as they were uncovered, as they refocused on the cactus. This was to test the quality of his depth perception, as well as check for such conditions as cross eye and lazy eye.

Satisfied that both of my lover's eyes were largely functional, if a bit nearsighted, Dr. Torrance went on to do a retinoscopy on him. This involved a device that used subjective refraction, that is input from the patient being tested, and was known as a phoropter. Looking like a giant eye mask with a lot of knobs and lenses, the function of the thing was to determine the strength of lens a person would need in order to have the best pair of glasses. With the phoropter at his face, the doctor had James stare at the eye chart on the wall again and tell him which lenses made the letters on the chart come through stronger. When the test was done the doctor made some notes and then told James that he would need a slightly stronger prescription of glasses.

"I need a new pair anyway," he remarked as he registered relief at the large lens machine being pulled away from his handsome face. "I want you, circus cutie, to help me pick a pair."

"I will, James love, never fear," I told him as I thought of all the times I'd been forced to endure the phoropter for my own nearsight. At such times, I thought of myself as "the woman in the iron mask."

Dr. Torrance rolled the phoropter aside and began doing the ophthalmoscopic examination. In preparation for this, he put eyedrops in both of my lover's eyes to dilate his pupils. Then he brought out a device called a direct ophthalmoscope. This was a hand-held illuminated 15X multi-lens magnifier that enabled the doctor to view the inside back areas of each of James' eyes, also known as the "fundus". This gave a critical view of his retina, blood vessels, and optic nerves. Right after this exam, the eye specialist pressed a button on a computer board and pictures of James' fundus came onto the screen. With their ruddy color and networks of canal like veins, each of these back views of his orbs looked like NASA shots of Mars or the blood red moon that occurs now and then, usually as the result of heavy forest fires or a total solar eclipse.

Next came the slit lamp examination where the ophthalmol- ogist had James rest his chin on the frame part of a machine whose main purpose was for looking into his eyes in the most minute detail. On the other side of the frame, Dr. Torrance looked through a microscope directly in both of his eyes.

This was followed by a perimetry or visual field test. Its func- tion was to measure all areas of James' eyesight, including his side or peripheral vision. For this exam, Dr. Torrance had him look into a bowl-shaped instrument, called a perimeter and keep on the look out for flashes of light that could appear in any direc- tion. He further told him that whenever he saw a flash, he was to press a button on a small control panel attached to the perimeter.

Lastly, was the intraocular pressure measurement test where James endured having more drops put in his eyes, anesthetic this time, and then placing his chin in a box like device that shot a puff of air into first one eye than the other.

When all of the tests were done, the doctor looked at the results and smiled at us with a beneficent smile on his broad tanned face.

"I'm happy to say, James, that aside from slightly worse myopia, both your eyes are perfect. Not even a hint of a cataract, like you feared. You will need a new prescription for glasses though," he said as he showed the written results of the tests to James.

I looked at the fundus photos. They indeed did look like a red moonscape. We thanked the doctor with a handshake.

"James, why don't you go look at our new eye glasses?" added the stout doctor as he waved his chubby hand in the direction of the wall where all of the sample spectacle frames were hanging, begging to be tried on for size. "We can have a pair ready for you in less than a week.

"No thanks, sir. I have no permanent address right now, so it wouldn't work. Could I please have a prescription from you though and copies of the results of my exam," asked James.

"I can do that for you," replied the ophthalmologist as he returned to the exam room. In a few minutes he was back with a prescription note and a sheet of papers, including the lunar-like fundus pictures.

We thanked him and the kindly little receptionist and then left for our car. I would be driving since James' eyes were still dilated and it was hard for him to see. I was not the best driver in the world, but I could get from here to there in a vehicle safely if the times called for it. James pulled Taffy unto his lap. She was acting agitated from having been left by herself for so long, but he calmed her down. He gave me a kiss for luck, then I started the car and we were on our way.

By then it was late afternoon, but still sweltering. Thank
God for the air conditioner that had been going steady all day
making the inside of our car as cool and cozy as a cucumber on
wheels. The Festiva's stereo sound system was playing James'
America rock group CD and their beautiful, enigmatic melody
"Horse With No Name" was pouring through the car's interior
like the stirring desert wind. It's very words seemed to fit our
journey very well. Although I couldn't hear it with all of the
windows rolled up, I was sure that the air around us was full of
sound. Not just of the wind, but of the songs of various birds.
Now that the sun was going down in a blaze of crimson glory,
all of the desert's citizens were starting to come out of hibernation. And rocks were everywhere to be seen, some pebbles
and some imposing boulders, but all of them having in common
being worn smooth by the sand blasting wind. However, our
horse certainly had a name – Ford Festiva! When that song
ended, on came the group's guitar rift rich, but cynical "Pigeon
Song". This tune never appeared on the music charts for probably obvious reasons. How could a song about a guy killing
his pet pigeon and dog, blowing up a railway, and destroying
his own farm, all in the name of wanting to "feel free", ever
be popular. Even so, James and I had to admit that it did have
a good melody and Dan Peek's strumming and vocals were at
their very best throughout the otherwise tritely morbid song. It
was also a hint of what was around the next corner.

As I took the car down highway 92 to the town of Bisbee,
we drove past the terraced pit remains of the former copper
mine known as the Lavender Pit. I admired its Colosseum-like
roughly circular reaches as they were bathed in the increasingly
bright light of a full moon.

"We will stop there and do a tour of that place when it's daylight," promised James whose eyes were starting to recover from
the dilating eye drops. "It is quite impressive and has a rich

lode of history." The dark of night was settling over the brush studded hills and Taffy had dosed off contentedly on his lap.

"I bet it has, cute guy. When I think of a copper mine I think of the one near Midway, British Columbia that I used to visit as a kid. It was in the nearby town of Greenwood and the remains of that one are up in the mountains. This mine was started sometime in the late 1880s. There was also a smelter and its red brick chimney stands to this day. This smelter was built in 1901 and the whole copper enterprise was booming until the war-inflated copper industry caused it to fold in 1918," I said as I eased the car past a truck full of what looked like wooden boxes containing various vegetables. I tried to keep my eyes and my attention on the road ahead, but it was hard for me to not lapse into nursing on memories of my happier early days in Canada.

"I've heard of that mine, circus chick. And gold and silver were also mined and smeltered there. Which reminds me, we should go gold panning together sometime. I now of all the rich deposits around here," added James invitingly.

"We will do that, cute guy. I used to go gold panning with the folks in all the back woodsy lakes and streams every weekend up there in ole BC. I even found a nugget or two, so did my mom and dad," I said as I looked at him with a grin. Then I turned the corner, waited for the stop light, and continued on.

"I can tell you're going to be a great prospector, Bonnie love."

"Thanks, I even learned how to work an old sluice box. There were gold claims all over the area where I was living then."

"So why didn't your family strike it rich?"

"Not lucky I guess."

"Is that so? Well, here's something that might make you luckier," as he said that, my lover fished out a little trinket that

84

was the image of a white cat with a raised paw. "Please take this, sweet cheeks. This is the Japanese diety, Maneki-neko who's thought to bring good luck and lots of money. I got her from my dad, Max, who got it from a Japanese prisoner during the war. Seems the guy was grateful to him for saving him from a crowd of GIs who wanted to beat him to a pulp after he was disarmed and captured. Anyway, I want you to have it, Bonnie."

As James said this, he tenderly placed the porcelain good luck cat in my hand. I leaned over and thanked him with a kiss as I pocketed the charm. When I returned my eyes to the empty desert road, it had gotten a lot darker, so we both decided to find a place to bed down for the night.

On the outskirts of Bisbee a sign came into view featuring lodging and something more – a pigeon farm. Not surprisingly, the outfit was called Gina's Pigeon Roost. On seeing the sign, James sat suddenly forward. At the same time, Taffy came awake with a soft *hoohoohoo* sound.

"I know this chick. She has the biggest pigeon breeding business in this part of America and some really nice guest cabins. I interviewed her in 1978," announced James.

"Then let's stay the night here. You can introduce me to her," I said as I parked the car in the lot beside the registration office.

"You bet I will, Bonnie love," said James as we left the car. He handed Taffy over to me.

"You better take her now. I think she wants her mommy," said James with a laugh.

My monkey gave out a few cooing sounds as I gathered her into my arms and the three of us made our way to the registration building. Although they were hard to see in the dark, I could tell that there were murals of pigeons painted on its sides. When we entered the office, we were met by a spry, still attractive lady in her mid-70s.

"Ah, Miss Santa Rosa. You remember me. I'm James Schön-hausse. I did an article on you once," my lover explained cheerfully as he nodded his head briefly.

"Why yes, I recall you, James, and your fine article too. Welcome back to my humble pigeon farm," beamed the fine lady as she shook his hand. Then her gaze turned to me and Taffy.

"And who might this pretty young lady be, James. She has an adorable pet monkey," as Gina Santa Rosa said this, Taffy reached over and took her hand. The lady clasped her furry little paw tenderly.

"This here is my girlfriend, Bonnie, and her monkey, Taffy. They make quite a fun pair to travel with," said James with a mixture of pride and humor.

"I'm happy to meet you, Miss Santa Rosa. I like it that you raise pigeons. I had a pet pigeon when I was a young child. I called her 'Pidge', I explained with a laugh.

"That's cute, Bonnie. Now, what can I do for you guys? If you stay overnight I can show you my birds in the morning. I have both Birmingham Rollers and Parlor Rollers. You see, Birmingham rollers can roll or somersault, backwards in rapid, tight rotations. They can do this while flying or while resting on the ground. Parlor Rollers, on the other hand, can't fly at all. They roll, turn their somersaults on the ground," related Miss Santa Rosa as she gestured to a wall containing awards her birds had won in competitions based solely on how far they could roll.

"That is interesting, but we'll have to wait and see a demonstration tomorrow morning. Tonight we're all tired and just need a place to sleep," explained James with a yawn. Taffy yawned at the same time too, which amused all three of us humans.

"You can rent cabin number four. The price is $140 for two people for an overnight stay and it has a nice view of the hills and a lake close by," Pets of all kinds are welcome, including your little one. What's her name, by the way?" invited Miss Santa Rosa as she offered us a pen shaped like a pigeon.

"Taffy, Miss Santa Rosa and we'll take number four," agreed James who paid for the three of us to bunk in the small wooden guest house.

The transaction complete, we each shook her hand and then took the key for rental number four. Before bedding down, we unloaded some items we would need from the car, like clothes, food, and grooming items, and put them in the little off-white unit. After eating a bite, I put Taffy to bed. I spent the rest of the night, rattling the bed springs with my husky beloved as the pigeons roosting in their kit box pen houses close by soothed us with their chorus of cooing.

After waking up the next morning we had breakfast with our hostess on the porch of her dove gray stucco house. As my lover, Taffy, and I dined on southwestern style omelets with pancakes, and coffee, our hostess told us more about herself and her profitable hobby of raising roller pigeons. I glanced over at the lady's 12-foot-by-8-foot breeding pens that housed pairs of birds. Near them were the 4-foot-by-8-foot kit boxes that were permanent pigeon roosts.

"You have quite a going concern here with your pigeons. I remember the day I interviewed you and how you let me watch a couple of them perform," remarked James with that grin he always wore when he was trying to draw someone out, verbally.

"Yes, they did put on quite a show for you that afternoon and they were both champions that had competed in the National

Birmingham Rollers Club. As you know, Some of my other birds have won prizes at the World Cup which is held annually at a different location around the world," related Miss Santa Rosa with a touch of pride.

"Your birds competed in several different countries, haven't they, Gina?" prodded James.

"They have performed in England, Sweden, Germany, Poland, and France and got top honors." replied the bird fancier as she finished off her coffee and poured more for every one but Taffy who was enjoying her orange juice.

"Those are achievements to be proud of, Gina! You have really gone forward with your success, both as a breeder and as a handler," said James as he sipped his coffee thoughtfully.

"When you raise rollers, the bird's living quarters are always divided into several compartments. Separation pens are used to divide the sexes during the nonbreeding season, pairs of birds reproduce in a breeding pen. Each pair has a nest box, where they lay eggs and raise their young. Competition birds are housed together, as a team, in kit boxes. The boxes also are the point from which the birds take flight – comparable to a runway, with clearance – and where they return. I own about 155 birds, most of them are the Birmingham variety. I prefer to breed 12 pairs of birds at a time," continued the woman with the dove gray hair. After she related this, she finished off her own breakfast with a long drink of coffee and then added. "James, would you and your girls like some more breakfast?"

"No, but thank you kindly. It was delicious and I enjoyed hearing some more about your pigeons," replied my husky lover.

"Both of us are full," I chimed in while wiping Taffy's mouth.

At that juncture, our hostess cleared the outdoor picnic table and had another treat in store for us. Squinting in the rising Arizona sun, our heads tilted back and scanning the sky, we watched as a couple of her prize birds performed their aerial feats.

"If it's not windy, they go so high you can't even see them," explained Miss Gina Santa Rosa. "The only time they leave is if something is chasing them. But they always come back, you can depend on that!"

As the pair somersaulted in the clear desert air, Taffy clapped her hands and squealed with delight. At the end of the Roller bird show, we told Miss Santa Rosa farewell and thank you for the wonderful time.

"Always remember," remarked James with wry humor. "The bird's the word." All three of us laughed heartily at that remark, since he was quoting a line from The Trashmen's goofy 1963 hit "Surfin Bird".

With our bellies full of mirth and a good breakfast, we were on our way to Bisbee with James in the driver's seat again. When we arrived there I noticed that it was a small, but impressive town with many tall brick Victorian-style buildings surrounded by tall, brush dotted hills. Further in the background were the Mule Mountains, as gray and wrinkled as an elephant's hide. James stopped for gas and we took some pictures. Then we got back on highway 80 headed for New Mexico. Before crossing the state line, the three of us came upon a most intriguing site. It was a ranch fence with worn-out old cowboy boots sheathing every post.

"Ha ha. Now, Bonnie love, that is a symbol for sex in leather and wood," remarked James as he slowed down to get a better look at what he deemed was a western erotic display. But I had different notions.

89

"Really! It's about as sexy as those pairs of rotten old tennis shoes I sometimes see looped over telephone poles and wires to frighten away birds. Has nothing to do with sex!" I said with a snotty grin.

"Aw, sweet cheeks! Where's your sense of humor?" remarked James who could tell that he was "getting my goat". Taffy was jabbering delightedly as she gazed at the line of boots with fixed interest.

"In the nearest branding pit. I've heard the real reasons cowboys put boots on fences have nothing at all to do with sex. They put up a pair every time they lose a beloved horse or hired hand. Sometimes, it's to let people know that the boss is home. Often it's just because they're so fond of their boots they'd rather make them a display on a fence than throw them away once they get too worn to wear. Some do it out of tradition, because they've seen other cowboys put up boots like that," I explained, proud of myself that it was now my turn to share some little known facts.

"But I knew all that, Bonnie love," said James, not to be outdone. He followed that revelation with a kiss and all was well for me again.

Chapter Nine

We gazed at miles and miles of desert as our little Festiva forded its way into New Mexico. It was still hot that early September, so we traveled mostly through the cooler northern regions of the state. James and I took Taffy through the dark recesses of Carlsbad Caverns where a bat flapped past her startling the daylights out of her. We walked the length and breadth of unearthly Shiprock with its towering pillars of stone. The three of us skipped through the pristine dunes of White Sands National Monument where we also enjoyed lunch at a shaded picnic table.

As the month drew to a close and cooler temperatures began to predominate, James braved doing a stop over in Silver City, the town that for him held a web of so many foreboding memories.

"I need some of the hair of the silver fanged dog that bit me," said my broad shouldered lover jokingly as we stopped for lunch at Silver City's fine Mexican eatery – El Gallo Pinto.

"And I need to bite a taco. Also, you can face the torments of your past better on a full stomach," I told James with a playful wink.

We left the car with Taffy and entered the restaurant's swinging doors. A melodious blast of Mexican music poured out to us as a pretty, dark-haired waitress informed us that the place was pet-friendly. Beaming she led us over to a table and gave me and

James menus. Both of us ordered chicken tacos. James ordered his with extra hot sauce. I ordered a chicken taco salad for Taffy. As we dined, the lively, accordion-accompanied singing in Spanish continued, but not so loudly that it interfered with me and my lover talking.

"So how are you feeling, James honey?" I asked him between spicy mouthfuls.

"Better than I expected to feel. Coming back here was a good idea. It made me face my old fears and bad memories from way back," he told me with a smile revealing growing inner peace.

"That's wonderful. Does that mean that Silver City no longer has bad vibes for you? That all is forgiven?"

"Not entirely, but its a start. I'll need an expungement, remember? And you and I need to do a serious talk, sweet cheeks."

"Well, cute guy, talk away. I'm ready to listen."

"Not here, Bonnie love. Some place more private and with the right kind of atmosphere."

"Okay, where then?"

"After we eat here, come with me to the mountains."

The three of us finished our lunch and then made for the Black Range mountains some 150 miles away. When we arrived, the late afternoon sun was bathing the craggy, tree-studded hills in a last burst of mellow light. James parked the car and led me and Taffy up a steep mountain pathway. As we trod the dusty trail, I happened to look up and see flying over the tops of the ridged hills what at first I took to be a large bat. But when it flew closer and roosted on a nearby butte, I was stunned to see that it looked like something else and something that was highly unlikely to be seen anywhere on Earth, at least in this day and age. No bat has a 20 foot wing span and no bat is ever that scaly or has a long powerful leathery beak.   James, as amazed as I was grabbed me by the arm and pointed it out to me in the still strong daylight.

"Bonnie, do you see that!" he gasped.

"Yes, I see it. It looks like a..a.." I said in a near whisper of awe.

"Pteranodon!"

"B...But they're supposed to be extinct. Aren't they?"

"Aren't they?"

My response was to hand Taffy over to James and fish my camera out of my handbag. Just then the prehistoric bird, beast, or whatever it was left its rocky perch and soared over us with a loud squawk that was different from any bird call I'd ever heard before. Taffy who'd been shivering with fear and clinging to James, started to scream.   James did his best to comfort her. With a quick aim of my Kodak, I was able to capture a photo of it in mid-flight as it winged its way over the trees and into a valley where it disappeared in spite of its great size.

"Maybe that really was one of those Pteranodon flying dino-saurs," I commented as I put my camera back in my handbag. "I've heard various stories of people finding dinosaurs in remote areas all over the world. I don't believe they're all extinct."

"Also, have you heard of rifts in time?" asked James as he continued to cuddle Taffy who was beginning to settle down.

"Yes I have and I believe in them."

"We could have seen the affects of one right now. Maybe a

time rift opened and that lizard bird flew right through."

"Sure, why not."

I took Taffy back and the moment she was back in my arms, she stopped quivering. James led us up to a cave. The air around us was cooling down up there and the wind was picking up, so James had donned a wool poncho woven with red, black, and tan Apache designs. Lovingly, he draped one just like it around me and Taffy and kissed me.

"Bonnie love, these ponchos aren't just for warmth. They're for good magic. These mountains are also called "The Devil's Mountains" or "Sierra Diablo" and are said to be full of powerful energy, both positive and negative. What's more, they're close to the Gila Cliffs where I provoked these energies with my folly. But the design on these outfits we're wearing was made by a powerful Apache shamaness I once knew and provide us with protection from the negative energies and act as a magnet for the positive energies. Bonnie, we must talk, but there's something I need to do first. Just stay where you are with Taffy and don't move. You'll be fine," James explained while building a fire in which he burned a bundle of fragrant smudge sticks.

Watching the rippling flames and smelling the aromatic smoke from the small bonfire caused me to doze off on the rock where I was reclining. Taffy was sound asleep. James mumbled a few words I couldn't make out. My heart jumped as a bunch of sparks flew out of the flames, then my eyes were suddenly wide awake as I saw, or thought I saw, a headless bird, possibly a hawk, leap out of the smoke carrying a writhing snake on its back. I naturally doubted the reality of what was I was seeing, even though I had seen something almost as strange earlier in the shape of a dinosaur bird and had the picture on my camera to prove it. But this sight was just too weird to be real under any circumstances. Still, I felt it would have been unwise for me to scream. So I held Taffy close and didn't make a sound as I observed the nightmarish creatures vanish out the cave's mouth, while James sat before the bonfire as though in a trance.

I blacked out.

When I came too, I was in James' arms and he was smiling down at me blissfully. At my feet was Taffy playing with a corn cob doll dressed as an Apache squaw. I was feeling drained and somewhat out of it.

"What...what was that! I feel like I passed out or something," I stammered glancing around.

For a brief moment, I glanced over at the fire expecting to see something demonic jump out of it again. All I saw were leaping flames that even seemed to be casting benign shadows. Now and then I fancied I saw the shadows of a dancing Indian or a prancing coyote.

"I took you on a healing vision quest with me, Bonnie love. I used an Apache ritual that's thousands of years old and I believe that it purged us both of our inner demons," said James as he raised me gently to my feet.

"Is that what that thing was?" I asked shakily, remembering the awful headless bird carrying the rattler.

"What kind of thing did you see, circus chick?"

"It...it was a headless bird, my guess is it was a hawk and it was leaping around with what appeared to be a rattle snake on its back."

"I saw it too. That was the embodiment of all the evil in this mountain range, but also all of the evil that's been shadowing both of us throughout our lives. Where'd it go?"

"Out of the cave as far as I could tell."

"Good, then we're completely free of it. I feel like a bad weight has been lifted from me. I feel free."

"I have to admit that I feel much better now too, cute guy."

Indeed my initial dazed condition was starting to ease into a state of growing emotional uplift. We kissed. Then as Taffy cuddled her corn dolly and fell asleep, James and I made love on the cave floor with a passion that was truly liberated. On the wall above us, illuminated in the camp fire's flames, was a stylistic phallic pictograph done in red ochre paints. As James entered me, I felt the Apache painting was a blessing on our union.

When our ardor was spent, a chorus of cave crickets serenaded me and my robust lover as I drifted off into the most peaceful sleep I had ever enjoyed. Soon I was dreaming. In this nocturnal vision, I wandered into another chamber of the cave and found a beautiful Apache Shamaness weaving on a primitive loom. I could see that she was making a colorful robe. When the fine, raven-haired lady was done with it, she stood up and slipped it over me.

"Your bridal dress, my dear, your maternity gown," she told me softly.

"Thank you, Weaver Queen," I told her nodding my head in gratitude.

A moment later, I came awake with James snoring softly beside me. I gave him a kiss and he came awake. We made love again and then we dressed. Before we left the cave, I noticed to my amazement an Apache robe beside me. It was identical to the one Weaver Queen had given me in my dream the night before. I was puzzled, but had experienced so many strange visions and events since joining my life to James that I didn't question it. With a smile, I showed the soft as a prairie cloud garment to him before folding it and putting it in my hand bag.

"That's beautiful!" he said with a hint of surprise in his sweet tenor voice. "Where and when did you buy that?"

"I didn't, cute muscle guy," I replied with a mysterious grin. "I just looked and there it was."

"Ha ha. Something that lovely wouldn't just appear out of nowhere, now would it, circus doll."

"I dreamed about a robe just like it last night. With all of the good vibes having been brought to life by your ritual and all of the bad ones chased away, maybe I dreamed it into existence."

"Hmmm. Maybe."

With that agreed on, James and I took Taffy out and all of us drained the dragon. Then we hopped in our car and returned to Silver City. Once there, we went to El Gallo Pinto for breakfast. James and I had a breakfast burrito and coffee, while Taffy munched on half of one and followed that up with a banana. When we were half-through with the morning meal, my brown-haired lover looked at me seriously through his gold-rimmed photograys. He had something important to say.

"Bonnie, sweet cheeks, when I got to know you a little, I decided that you weren't my type and that you just didn't inspire any romantic feelings in me at all. I believe I'm not in love with you. The problem is I seriously doubt I could ever love anyone again after Licia broke my heart," said James slowly and with emphasis.

"Does this mean 'Goodbye!' or let's just be friends? Because I won't tolerate either!" I cut in with fury as I rose from my seat with my fists clenched.

Beside me, Taffy was jabbering indignantly while making a move like she was about to throw her banana skin at him.

"Ha ha. Whoa, girlie! No, I'm not about to dump you by leaving you in the lurch or semi-dump you by demanding that our relationship decline to strictly platonic. No, either one would be a chicken shit thing for me to do to you and would hurt you immeasurably and I couldn't bare hurting you like that. You see, Bonnie, I like you, I enjoy your company, and I care deeply for you. So instead I'll propose, if you'll pardon the pun, to do something else," James said in a very kind, compromising voice, a voice eager to make peace with me.

"All right," I ventured, feeling growing relief as I sat back down and Taffy returned her attention to her stub of a banana. "What do you propose?"

"Just this, circus chick. Now let me see your left hand," he ordered with boyish whimsy. I shrugged my shoulders and reached out to him with my left hand. I thought I knew what he was leading up to and hoped in my heart that I was guessing correctly. James gently, but firmly took hold of my proffered hand and slipped a ring on my fourth finger. He followed that with a kiss on my hand, then on my lips.

"What I propose, Bonnie love, is marriage. Will you be Mrs. James Schönhausse?" my lover asked me tenderly, but earnestly.

"Yes, of course, cute guy!" I replied staring at the ring he just bestowed on me as though hypnotized by its glittering radiance.

It was a large diamond in a very antique silver setting comprised of roses and rose leaves.

"That was my mother's wedding ring. I have been intimately involved with other women, I was even married to one, but none of them were special enough to me to deserve the honor of having mom's ring. Only you, Bonnie love. That's how much you mean to me," said James as he gave me another kiss.

Beside me, Taffy was clapping her hands and giggling with approval in her own monkey way.

Eager to bind our union in the golden promise the ring symbolized, James bought a marriage license for us at the Silver City Court House. With this document in hand, he drove me 300 miles to Chaco Canyon. On the way, he hired a preacher and together my love and I spoke our wedding vows by the stone walls of Fajada Butte where an 11th Century pictograph depicted the supernova of 1054 with a moon, a star, and a hand.

The whistling of the canyon wind through the history-rich structure's nooks and gaps was all the wedding song I wanted or needed. Of course, I wore my dream wedding dress. Of course, Taffy was my flower girl standing beside me and James with a little woven basket full of wildflowers. On her furry little head was a wreath of similar blossoms.

I never felt happier and my joy was increased and added to by surprise when our friend Addy appeared on the wedding scene. Right away, James appointed him best man. When the ceremony was done, the blond stunt biker kissed the bride, meaning me, and then gave me and James a wedding present of $200 each.

Chapter Ten

James and I spent a blissful, fulfilling honeymoon in our tent at Chaco Canyon. We made hot, arduous love all through the night as Taffy nodded off to dreamland. At some point, James and I fell asleep, satisfied in each other's arms and with our bodies entwined. But just as we began to drift into sleep, my husband and I were startled awake by the feeling that the land all around us was shaking heavily.

"Wha...what's going on?" I blurted out, concerned that we might be experiencing an earthquake.

"I don't know. Let's go find out," said James with a cross between curiosity and uneasiness.

We quickly slipped on some robes and I grabbed hold of Taffy who had been chattering and running around excitedly ever since the shakes started. Just then, the earth heaving suddenly stopped and was replaced by the bellow of a train whistle. James looked at me with a smile that said, now we know what was shaking the ground. Sure enough, as soon as we left the tent, we saw before us a medium-sized locomotive. It was nothing less than a Santa Fe Northern 3751 that had been outfitted with passenger cars and a rear car with an observation deck. The mighty machine was making the screeching and groaning sounds trains of their make always do when they are stalling.

"I didn't know there was a train track here, cute guy," I said with quiet awe as I admired the locomotive illuminated in the midnight blue darkness only by the light flooding its cars and pouring from its headlight.

"I didn't either. I guess we were both so drunk with passion and beer last night that we hardly noticed anything but each other, sweet cheeks. But that's quite a rattler, isn't it?" Commented James whose light-brown eyes were taking in the whole length and breadth of it.

"Rattler" is a common slang word for "train" especially in Utah where he spent most of his early childhood.

"Indeed it is," I agreed, holding Taffy even closer.

It began to rain. Not enough to get any of us wet, more like a gentle sprinkle or mist. Just then, the door of the nearest boxcar opened and a small metal platform slid into position. Who should appear out of the door then but our elusive friend, Addy Geisst. What's more, he was wearing a white train conductor's uniform, visored cap and all. He was jauntily swinging and old-fashioned kerosene lamp in his hand.

"Hi guys, all aboard!" he called out invitingly.

James took me by the hand and we walked over to the small metal platform where Addy was standing. Taffy reached out to him and jabbered a "Hello!". Just at that moment a halo of fire flies swarmed past his blond head.

"On board for where, Addy?" James demanded to know.

"Why, all over New Mexico on the most exciting tour ever! Are you comin'?" asked Addy like a showman inviting a family to watch a three ring circus.

"Sure, why not, Addy. I'm in the mood for a top-of-the-line

adventure," said James, catching his excitement. "I also want to know how the great motorcyclist got hold of a train like this one."

"Me too, Addy. This is quite a loco locomotive," I agreed, suddenly wondering about the train myself.

"All of your questions will be answered, James and Bonnie. But first, come and take a seat. The ride of your life is about to begin," said Addy as I stepped up the steel platform behind James.

Just before going into the passenger car, I briefly glanced behind me and noted the night-draped landscape. The rain had stopped and now a full moon and a canopy of brilliant stars were out. It felt warm out, more like spring than autumn. Indeed, there were flowering cactus and blooming yucca round about. So unusual for October. Birds sang in the trees. Some flower petals fell through the air. For a second, I wondered if I might be dreaming, but I made up my mind to enjoy what I was experiencing to the fullest, be it dream or reality.

The train started up with a jerk that pulled me away from my musings as the springlike scenery began moving past me with increasing speed. As James hauled me the rest of the way in, I caught a glimpse of somebody waving me goodbye. It was a scarecrow in a sombrero and Mexican shawl standing in a garden of columbine and heartleaf arnica. The warm breeze was making its wooden stake "arm" move in a wave-like motion.

"Hurry in here, Bonnie, before you and Taffy fall out on the ground!" exclaimed James as he grabbed me by the waist and pushed me into the parlor car.

"Thanks, cute guy," I said with an embarrassed laugh. "I got a little distracted by that scarecrow out there. He seemed to be waving at us."

"Ha ha. He was seeing us off on a spirited journey," said James in a tone that was both lighthearted and mysterious.

I sat Taffy down and we followed my man as he was led over to a row of seats by our tall long-haired host.

"Please get comfy, guys. I have to return to the engine car, but I'll be back to visit with you shortly. We have a lot to talk about. By the way, this is Kohan Pelli. Kohan, meet my newly wed friends, James and Bonnie, and their furbaby, Taffy," said Addy as he smiled in the direction of a tall, angular, handsome, Apache fellow in blue jeans and a home-spun grasshopper motif shirt. His black hair stuck out whimsically in spiky wild dread-locks. I guessed him to be a traveler like James and me since he was wearing a small knapsack on his back.

"Greetings and congratulations, James and Bonnie. What a cute monkey you have there too. Here, let me play you a little wedding song in celebration," said Kohan as he picked up a flute and favored us with a melody as sweet and lovely as the spring zephyr breezing outside.

James and I thanked him and took our seats. Taffy sat beside me and played with the string of my handbag. Just then, Addy returned.

"Would any of you guys like a snack. We have every kind of taco and every variety of soft drink. There's also beer," our conductor friend informed us.

"I'll pass on the beer, I've already had too many tonight. But two beef tacos and a Dr. Pepper would really hit the spot. How about you, Bonnie love? Want a beer or a taco or both?" suggested James with a gentle nudge on my shoulder.

"I'll have a root beer instead of a real beer and I want a beef taco with my James here. Taffy's hungry too, so if your chef could make a plain tortilla and put some banana slices on it for her, I'd be really happy," I said as my monkey softly chattered as though in agreement with my food choices.

"Yes to all of that, guys. So, what would you like, Kohan?" continued Addy glancing over at the cinnamon complected flute player.

"I'll take a coke and an Indian taco," replied Kohan crossing his slender fingers together.

An Indian taco is made by taking a piece of frybread, instead of a regular tortilla, and filling it with the usual taco ingredients. Frybread is a flat dough bread, fried or deep-fried in oil, short-ening, or lard.

"Comin' right up, said Addy who went to a microphone and called all of our orders into it, putting in a chicken taco and a beer for himself.

With our late night meal being prepared, Addy came over and sat with me, Taffy, and James. We chatted together as Kohan played another lilting tune for us on his flute. At one point, Taffy got down from her seat and danced to his music for the amuse-ment of us all.

"My monkey likes your flute playing," commented James with a laugh.

She broke off her dancing and regained her seat where she began looking out a window. I left the men to converse and joined her. Outside it was gently sprinkling again. We rode past an archway made entirely of flowers and right beneath it was a department store featuring a colorful display of more flowers, Indian rugs, baskets, and large faux butterflies that actually flut-tered around behind the huge display window.

"How beautiful and springy!" I said out loud to Taffy who seemed entranced by the bird-sized plastic butterflies.

The train passed the store and moved towards the outskirts of town which was populated by a few houses. Just then, my attention was caught by a foursome of smartly dressed Mexican waiters who did a lively flamenco dance as they placed a table in front of us and prepared to serve us our meals. The young men's sense of balance was breath-taking as they spun, tapped their toes, and clicked their castanets, all the while laying down our food and pouring our drinks without one spill or mishap. Taffy squealed with joy and clapped her hands. In the background someone was playing the upbeat romantic strains of flamenco guitar music as the dancers whirled and tapped. They even treated us to a ranchero song in Spanish.

"Los tacos, los tacos en la primavera,
  Sentarse, relajarse, vamos a alimentación piensos.
  Los tacos, los tacos en la primavera,
  Sentir el amor y comer el relleno, el relleno."

(Tacos, tacos in the spring,
  Sit down, relax, we'll feed you, feed you.
  Tacos, tacos in the spring,
  Feel the love and eat your fill, your fill.)

Kohan, who had joined the rest of us at our table, picked his flute back up and added its high, sweet tones to the waiters' lively song. James, who knows Spainish well, joined in with his harmonica. When their serving task was done, the four singer/dancers added a final flourish of placing a terra cotta vase full of datura and yarrow flowers – a pageant of white and purple – in the middle of our banquet. They also placed a crown of yarrow on my and Taffy's heads and then tap-toed and spun their way out of the parlor car as quickly and lithely as they'd tap-toed and spun in. The food they had delivered smelled marvelous. Addy prayed over it and we all dug in as the rain began to beat against the boxcar's windows with harder and swifter rhythm.

"Bonnie and James," said Addy sipping his beer thoughtful-ly, "I brought you both here, not only to celebrate your happy union, but to clear some mysteries up once and for all. And don't worry about baring your souls in front of Kohan, he's very understanding and good about keeping secrets."

Instantly, everyone's attention was riveted on our tall blond host as he continued his dialogue in a low confidential tone. Even little Taffy became hushed as she nibbled her banana taco.

"You have all heard about my death last year. It wasn't faked. I really did die but I've been allowed to return to earth to act as guardian angel for you two and as the grim reaper for somebody else," revealed Addy while putting the tips of his fingers together pensively.

"For who!" asked James leaning towards him.

"For your brother, Maximilian, but others as well," answered Addy as James flopped back in his seat with a gasp.

I took hold of his hand consolingly, as our friend who was turning out to be an angel of some sort, went on with his shock-ing revelations.

"You remember the night I hitched a ride with you, James, and you dropped me off at that gas station. Well, it was my mission to collect the soul of a guy who was working there that night. You see, I still race and do stunts, but my main job now is to take souls as God commands me too. Furthermore, because Maxi-milian was the one who took my life, it is now my duty to take his. But first I must give him a chance to repent."

"He never will," interjected James glumly.

"That is for God to decide and me to give him the opportunity to do," resumed Addy with a somewhat sad smile. "I will be racing him at that mountain soon and before, during, or after that event I will approach him with an offer for him to save his soul. As for you, Bonnie, I have a revelation for you too. It's about your former love, Wayne, the one that died on you so suddenly. I know how hard it was for you, girl, to lose him and his dog, Checkers, but he had to leave suddenly so that he could give guidance and comfort to me. You see, as violent and sudden as my death was, I badly needed an angel mentor and God chose Wayne. His dear little dog was taken too because, God knows, people in Heaven need their companion animals too. You might say truthfully that Checkers is your Wayne's mentor. Rest assured, Bonnie, both of them still love you very much and are looking out for you from their heavenly home. But they love you enough to let you go, to let you go and build a new life with James and Taffy."

After being told this, I buried my face in my hands and started sobbing. But I was crying tears of joy this time, not tears of grief. James wrapped his big arms around me while Taffy wreathed me in her tiny ones.

"And back to you, James. I know what a load of guilt you've been carrying all these years over Greg Strömson's death..."resumed Addy.

"Also, the adulterous affair I had with his wife, Lil. Please tell God for me how truly sorry I am and that I hope He forgives me," cut in James with a voice full of real pain.

"Rest assured, James, God forgave you for all that a long time ago," said Addy as he locked James' sorrowful brown eyes with a look of empathy. "And furthermore, you nor anyone else ever found out who actually killed Mr. Strömson. It was your brother who shot him and he did it for two reasons. To frame you, because he's always hated you that much, and also because your brother is secretly in charge of a huge gambling racket and that man owed him money, big time."

This time, it was James who was weeping when Addy was finished with the reveal. But he quickly steeled himself and wiped his tears away.

"Thank you, dear Addy, I do feel like a tremendous load has been lifted from me. Still I don't know whether I'm feeling sadness or gratification from being made aware that my psychopath brother is doomed," said my husband in a voice choked with emotions he was struggling to corral.

"James, you are stunned and a bit confused by all this which is very natural. But I believe you can clarify everything for yourself by taking one single, important step," suggested our spare, blond friend seriously.

"And what might that important step involve, Addy?" asked James as Kohan, Taffy, and I sat back and observed them both with an almost entranced interest.

"You must forgive your brother and bless him to his good. Think you're ready to do that, James?" continued Addy.

"Yes, I am now. This train ride has been a revelation on cranks and driving wheels," replied James with his broad face radiating a peace I had never on it before.

"Good, then there is a simple ritual you have to perform in order for this forgiveness to be lasting and a true healing between you two," Addy explained.

From there, he told my husky husband that he needed to write the words, "I hate you, Maximilian" on a piece of parchment with an old-fashioned ink pen from 1860 dipped in an ink well cast in the same year.

"Because that was the year when madness entered your family through your maternal Great-grandmother Hedwig. It was her madness that tainted your brother and even yourself to a lesser degree. But you can end this taint and at least make peace with him by doing as I instruct. Just write what I told you on this parchment and we'll take it from there," explained Addy further.

James nodded and wrote on the parchment. When he was done, Addy took the weathered looking piece of paper, glanced at it briefly, and then called over the intercom mike for the train to be temporarily stalled. The metal wheels grated and clanged as they came abruptly to a halt and all of us were pulled forward. Addy smiled as he led us out to the rear car with its railed observation deck.

When we stepped out, I noticed that the rain had stopped and the moon in all of its silvery luster was so close and bright the whole outdoor panorama was clear to be seen. We were up in the mountains and surrounded by a forest of tall pine trees. The ground was lush with a carpet of grass and here and there were clumps of white datura blossoms and yellow sagebrush which also looked white in the moonlight.

As Kohan began playing softly on his flute, Addy gave the parchment back to James.

"Crumple it and toss it, man," he told him.

Just as my husband made the cathartic missive up into a ball and then threw it, a slight tepid breeze full of plant fuzz wafted by. It bore the parchment out to an open meadow where it was trampled on by a pack of coyotes running through a nearby meadow. I noticed the group of dashing canines contained several pups barely old enough to be running with the rest. They kicked up the crumpled parchment which was caught by a passing roadrunner who flow off with it.

"She'll use that to build her nest," commented Kohan punctuating his words with musical bursts from his wooden pipe.

We believed him. The mystic musician was obviously wise about all things of nature. With the simple act of James releasing that piece of parchment he had written on to the winds of nature, he and I immediately felt that all of our troubles had been released as well. That our lives together would be a smooth rail ride from then on.

With a blissful smile showing that James' and my release had brought him some kind of resolution as well, Addy led the four of us back to the parlor car and ordered the engineer to start the train up again. With a mighty wail of its horn and the roaring of its engine, it was rolling down the track again. For the rest of the night, I was treated to scenery that was truly enchanting, the state living up to its nickname for me and my traveling partners.

Our locomotive rode trestles so lofty that I could see the tops of mountains and the tips of forest trees through their steel railing, tracks, and frames. Some of them were so steep that we rode them practically straight down. We traveled across brush crowned hills and down into flowered valleys rich with blooming yucca. We saw a herd of elk grazing in one of these open meadows. Rivers wriggled through the landscape, glittering and writhing in the moon's beams like silver snakes. Bathed in moon glow, the desert regions took on a magic of their own. Rolling sandy plains led to buttes and mesas skirted by soil and rocks.

But these deserts, far from being barren were teeming with multiple varieties of life. Blooming cacti graced its wind-swept confines along with bushes and tumbleweed, also in full flower. Various birds and animals darted in and out from behind the vegetation. Especially active were the many types of lizards and snakes that the cool of the evening had brought out from their daytime hibernation. As we steamed down the track through the arid Ojito Wilderness with its gnarled trees and clumps of indian paintbrush, we saw a large Great Basin Gopher Snake raise its spotted head and stick its tongue out at us as though in playful mockery. We all laughed when Taffy in turn stuck out her tongue at him.

James and I got to meet the train's engineer and fireman. Both were amiable young Mexicans. The engineer was a stout fellow named "Santos", while the fireman was a slim youth called "Fuego".

Near the end of the whole marvelous excursion and contrary to the laws of gravity, my husband and I followed Kohan with Taffy to the top of our parlor car where he used some items from his knapsack to build a fire and brew some coffee. He invited us to sit down on some blocks of wood, also miraculously retrieved from his magical knapsack, and drink some coffee with him from beat-up enamel cups. Even Taffy got some java that was diluted heavily with caramel creamer. The rain had started up again, but so gently and warmly that we barely noticed it. I felt cozy and insular around Kohan's fire.

"Nothing like some fresh coffee on a drizzly night like this," remarked the dark-eyed flute player as he poured a cup for himself and sat down to join us on an up-turned bucket.

"Thank you very much, Kohan. Two questions though. Why is it spring here? The last time I looked at the calendar it was October, getting way into fall. Also, how come we're sitting anchored here and not flying off the train top," asked James whose curiosity was hinged on a wish to know our mysterious friend better.

"James, some things are not meant to be analyzed or picked apart, just enjoyed," advised Kohan.

"Yes, cute guy. This may or may not be a dream. But whatever this ride is, just put your inquiring mind on hold and ride with it. You know you need to suspend your doubts sometimes, like we had to the other day when we saw that bird thing." I chimed in while hoping that if I was deep in a dream, I'd never wake up.

"What bird thing?" asked Kohan his obsidian eyes bright with mischievous curiosity.

"But it wasn't really a bird, it was more like a flying reptile. It looked for all the world like a prehistoric pteranodon. Bonnie, show him the picture," said James nodding in my direction.

On cue, I brought out my camera, clicked on its "review" button, and instantly the flying creature came on the LCD panel. I shared the picture of the bizarre leathery tan thing with both men.

"Hey guys, that's no winged dinosaur, its a nature spirit. They come and they go as they watch over us and they take many forms," said Kohan with a voice full of laughter at James' lapse into being too logical and technical in his views.

"Sort of like a guardian angel," I ventured, returning my camera to my handbag.

"Yes, more like that," replied Kohan.

"Ha ha. All right, I'll just chill out and go with the flow of this rain and this coffee," said James who realized he was outnumbered. "And speaking of coffee, could I have some more?"

"Here ya go, James," answered Kohan as he gave him a frothing second cup.

Then he reached into his knapsack and pulled out a handful of dice.

"Along with good coffee and company, nothing beats a good

game of dice on a wet drippy night. Care for a game of Bunco?" he offered plunking the dice down on a small collapsible table he had pulled out of his knapsack.

"I would like to play since dice games are metaphors for life. You never know what numbers will turn up for you, but if you keep rolling your chances of winning may get better and better," said James pulling up closer to the same wooden table.

"Count me in but only if Taffy can play too," I insisted as my monkey grabbed a dice and started to roll it around in her paws.

"Ha ha. It looks like she already is. Now guys in this version, the rules are like regular Bunco except we each play with two dice instead of three. So, grab your dice and let's get going. Whoever turns up the biggest number gets to go first," Said Kohan tossing his dice and then throwing them down.

James and I followed suit, with me also helping Taffy roll hers. Kohen got two fives, I got a four and a three, Taffy got a two and a one, while James got two ones – snake eyes! Obviously, Kohan would go first. We agreed that the target number would be 21. Each one of us would have a turn rolling and it was my job to keep track of our numbers each time we rolled and add them up. Whoever reached 21 first would be the winner. Kohan mentioned a prize. Just then James got one of his inspirations.

"This reminds me of the time I lost a glass eye to snake eyes," he said as he looked at the two dice "eyes" that one might fancy were staring back at him.

"Oh, and how did that happen, cute guy," I asked with a giggle.

"Yes, tell us," prodded Kohan as he turned up a two and a six on his second throw. "all right, Bonnie, you're next."

"It happened back in 1977," James began, "and I'd just gotten out of the service with an honorable discharge from a spinal injury. Leandra, my girlfriend at the time, had a brother named Lucky. He had lost an eye while serving in Vietnam and wore a glass eye. Because he was getting a new glass orb that time from the VA, he gave his old one to me, 'cause he knew how much I like weird things. Ha ha. Anyway, I took that glass eye and used my jewelry making tools and skills to turn it into a necklace pendant. The next evening Leandra and I were at this Silver City bar, could have been the Buffalo Bar Hall, I don't remember. I was wearing that glass eye necklace that night. We had a couple of whiskeys and then sat down at the table of a fellow who was playing dice for money. I played a few rounds with him while Leandra munched on beer nuts and watched amused. Thankfully, New Mexico has more tolerant laws regarding gambling, and often the police look the other way where social gambling is involved, or demand their cut. But that aside, I played the dice with this guy and he won every time. I was giving him every cent I had on me, until I was down to nothing and still owed him. 'I'll call it a deal,' he said, 'if you just throw in that crazy necklace." So I took it off my neck and gave it to him, sadder but wiser. I guess the experience was for teaching me an important lesson, I quit gambling for money from then on. So that's how I lost a glass eye to snake eyes."

"Trust me, friend, the last thing I'd want to do would be taking your money. We're all playing just for fun here. So what'd you get, Bonnie?" remarked Kohan who was eager to make all of us feel at home at his otherworldly campsite.

"Five," I said as I counted and scored.

Then it was James turn. He rolled and got eight. We played a couple of rounds and it was he who got the 21 winning score. With a flourish, Kohan gave him an amulet for his prize. It was eye-like and made of blue and white glass.

"I know this isn't quite like the real glass eye you lost, James.

But it's a magic piece that's made in Sicily and is supposed to protect you from the evil eye. Whether there's anything to that or not I'll let you be the judge, but I thought that since you like beads you might really like this," said Kohan placing the glass object of art in his hand.

"Thank you, dear Kohan, I do like it. I'll make a necklace of it and think of you every time I wear it," James said as he examined his glass eye-like prize admiringly.

"Oh, it's lovely!" I said thinking of similar ones I had seen in a craft shop in California during a trip in 1977.

Taffy chattered and reached for the protective glass "jewel". James give it to her to play with for a while, then we all drank more coffee. When the pot was empty, Kohan played us a few more tunes on his pipe, while I accompanied him with my accordion and James joined in with his harmonica. Taffy clapped her paws to the rhythm and danced a few times. When the train neared a mountain tunnel with a very low clearance, Kohan quickly put out his fire, grabbed all of his things into his knapsack and led us three back to our parlor car where Addy soon joined us. By then our marvelous train ride was nearing its end.

A few minutes later the locomotive had brought us back to our Chaco Canyon campsite. The first touches of dawn were starting to spark the horizon as James, Taffy, and I stepped off the platform and said our goodbyes to Addy who was standing framed by the cab doorway's golden light.

"Farewell and thank you for the awesome train ride, Addy," said James as he shook our friend's hand.

"No, James, thank you for joining me on this trip. You guys have been awesome company," remarked Addy as he patted Taffy on the head.

"Good luck with your stunt face-off with Maximilian, Addy. We'll be there to watch you beat that son of the Devil," I chimed in grabbing his hand in a good handshake.

"I know I will. And remember, girlie, this race is not about me outracing that lost pathetic man. It's about me giving him the chance to save his own soul," said Addy fixing me with a serious look in his eyes which were like twin blue flames boring into my soul.

James gave me a serious look too.

"Oh, how could I have forgotten that, Addy?" I replied feeling sheepish.

"Hey, it's all right, Bonnie," said my angelic friend, his tone becoming mellower. "And one more thing, you guys, understand that a train trip is a metaphor for the journey of life itself. It will teach you important lessons along the way, but most of all it is meant to be enjoyed."

We waved our final goodbyes as Addy disappeared back into the locomotive and its mighty wheels started moving forward. Up on the roof of our erstwhile parlor car was Kohan waving his final farewell. We waved back as his whole form turned to mist in the moonlight until all that remained was his hand holding his flute. Then that vanished too.

After we watched the train recede down the track from our view, James and I returned to our tent where we put Taffy to bed. My passionate husband and I then made love until the sun had chased the shadows of night from the heavens over Chaco Canyon. Then we dozed for a while and awoke to make love again.

Chapter Eleven

James, Taffy, and I stayed for a while at our Chaco Canyon campsite where fall had come in with all of its arid splendor. On October 5, we traveled back to North Dakota where we pitched our tent at the bottom of Sentinel Butte and waited for Addy and Maximilian to make their record breaking jump on the 8th.

Addy, angel that he was, had sent us free tickets to the event. As we waited for the evening of October 8 to arrive, James, Taffy, and I spent our time becoming better acquainted with our fellow spectators, most of whom had also chosen to camp out at the bottom of the Butte which happens to be one of North Dakota's highest elevation points. We also watched as the show's work crew built ramps for the racers and a stadium for the audience. Stadium lights were raised. James and I even found time to indulge in our hobby as amateur archaeologists. We found some fossilized remains of prehistoric phioplarchus whitei sunfish while inspecting the white and gray limestone crusting the top of the Butte.

"This variety of fish fossil can be found only in this region, Bonnie love. They and the p. sexspinosus are particular to this Butte and the other limestone formations surrounding it," explained James as he and I squatted to examine the fossil fish with closer scrutiny.

North Dakota fall evenings are beautiful. Sunset adds further splashes of red to a landscape already vibrant with gold and copper leafed trees and bushes. There is in the air a frosty sharpness, but just enough to make you feel invigorated.

The deep gold of an alpine glow had replaced the cinnabar hues of sundown when the time for the competition neared. Quick as a wink, the stadium lights flickered on as though trying to compete for dominance of the sky and landscape with the moon and rapidly appearing stars. Then key personnel began to arrive. First came the announcer and his staff. On their heels came the pit crews for both cyclists in their colorful jackets. Their pickups towed the contending motorcycles in shiny steel trailers – Addy's ethereal white Yamaha YZF-R6 and Maximilian's black as The Abyss Kawasaki ZX-6R. The moment they were parked, each five-member crew piled out and rolled the steel steed in their charge onto the ground where they fueled it and looked it over to make sure it was race worthy. Newspaper reporters and camera personnel had also put in their appearance, as James, the former newsman, was eager to point out to me.

Finally, the stunt racing stars themselves arrived on board their sleek, streamlined helicopters. The announcer went wild proclaiming from his high booth that "a contest unparalleled in the annuals of stunt cycling history" was about to take place.

Indeed it was. Daredevils before Addy Geisst and Maximilian Schön had rode their motorcycles over gaps of hundreds of feet. But only they were able to leap over hundreds of miles. Maximilian's record was 200 miles while Addy's 202. Even famed stunt biker Evel Knivel had only been able to do a leap of 141 feet for his top score. Now they faced the challenge of gunning their bikes over a 240 mile butte saddle. But they were both ready for it, gearing up in full throttle in fact.

When Addy leaped out of his 'coptor, he looked almost beatific in his all-white biking costume. The crowd cheered with a happy frenzy. Then Maximilian wearing a black leather jumpsuit that clung to him like a second skin, sprang from the door of his own whirlybird and faced the spectators with a mixture of arrogance and predatory menace. A mixed chorus then rang out from the audience. Some cheered, many booed.

At that point, a security person invited James and me to leave our seats in the bleachers and follow him over to where the two stunt bikers were preparing for their combination race and leap. A formidable-sized crowd was already gathering around the two men, clamoring for autographs and handshakes. Used to handling crowds, our muscular friend and his security guard cohorts were able to form a human wall, like Moses parting The Red Sea, so that James and me holding Taffy were able to have an exclusive pre-event visit with Addy and Maximilian.

"I'm sorry, brother, for all the trouble that's passed between us," said James' tall, lanky brother with unexpected contriteness.

"I'm sorry too, Max. I realize now that it wasn't all your fault," admitted my husband as he gave his younger brother a hug.

Maximilian seemed to lose some of his demonic edge at that moment as he released James and shook hands with me.

"And what a sweet, lovely wife you have here, James. Welcome to the Schönhausse Family," said Maximilian with an admiring smile.

"I'm proud to have you as a brother-in-law, Max," I said feeling great inner joy at witnessing a healing of deep family wounds.

The two brothers and I laughed as Maximilian playfully put his racing helmet on Taffy's tiny furry head. Instantly, she seemed to be swallowed up by it. My monkey started in with a volley of confused chattering so Maximilian removed his headgear and gave her a stick of string cheese.

But then, he turned to his rival, whom he'd been ignoring the whole time, and his entire aspect changed.

"As for you, Addy, I'm going to beat you down to the dirt. You'll eat my dust and some bushes and rocks to go with it" said the black-clad daredevil with a hateful sneer.

"I say, may the best man win and to the victor go the spoils, or rather, the trophy cup. So why don't we shake on that, Maximilian?" asked Addy hopefully.

"Never, I'd rather shake hands with the Devil himself! In fact, I'd much prefer the Devil!" Maximilian declined vehemently.

"Suit yourself," replied Addy shrugging his shoulders with a disappointed frown.

James and I both felt taken aback by his brother's brash defiance, so we wished them both the best of luck and, with help from the security people, found our way back to our places on the bleachers.

The announcer then began a play by play broadcast as Addy and Maximilian climbed on their motorcycles and revved them up while waiting for the signal to go. Minutes later, the signal was given while a pretty black girl in a bright-orange fall shift dress dropped the checkered flag. Like avenging angels Addy and his competitor were off with a roar of their cycles' hellbent for leather engines. With increasing speed, the stunt riders poured on the gas as they made their way up a winding 600 foot path to the sandstone and bush crowned top of Sentinel Butte's left plateau. Between that and the right plateau lay the 240 mile long saddle, yawning like the hungry mouth of Hell. On the way up there, Maximilian tried many times to run Addy off the path, but the white-garbed biker from Nebraska was too quick for him and dodged and outran him every time.

When they both reached the ramp that would help them build up speed for the climactic jump, they were running side by side for a split second. During that brief juncture, I saw Addy appear to turn his head and say something to Maximilian. In response the dark-clad rider shook his head and tore up the ramp like a man possessed. But Addy gunned his motor and soon caught up with him. They sped off the ramp and into the open air with rocks, trees, and bushes a long ways beneath them. Just then, as I, James, and everyone else watched with breathless fascination, something shocking and totally unexpected happened. For less than an instant, Addy and Maximilian soared exactly parallel as though their bikes were suspended above the saddle in defiance of the laws of gravity. Then there was a flash of fire and they were gone, vanished without a trace. All around me the crowd roared and shrieked with consternation.

"A tragedy has happened, friends. It appears that our heroes' motorcycles have collided in midair and then exploded!" the announcer was shouting.

But I knew what had happened. Addy had offered Maximilian the chance to save himself and the stubborn fool had refused, remaining hostile to the end. So Addy was left with no other choice but to take his soul on to whatever fate awaited it.

Touched by the full impact of knowing that, I clung to Taffy and cried. Soon, James was clinging to both of us and crying too.

Chapter Twelve

Immediately following the fiery disappearance of Addy Geisst and Maximilian Schön, a thorough investigation was initiated. Many persons were questioned by the police, including me and James since we were very close to both men. The whole area of the rock covered and bush overgrown Sentinel Butte was looked over with great zeal and scrutiny for remains, both human and motorcycle. However, not so much as a brake rod or a bone was found. In the end, the law authorities, both federal and state, were forced to come to one single, final conclusion – the two stunt racers had collided that night of October 8, 2013 in a mid-air explosion so intense that all traces of them and their machines were burned up without leaving a trace behind. Many ordinary folk insist that the biking rivals survived the crash and are hiding out somewhere to this very day. I believe that they, in a sense, are closest to the truth.

But even though no bodies nor wreckage had been found, the friends and families of both tragic men insisted on having funeral services for them. James and I went to each one to pay our respects – Addy's in Omaha, Nebraska and Maximilian's in Dayton, Utah. Both were held on days in early December with a drizzling mixture of snow and rain seeming to mirror the tears pouring down the chilled cheeks of everyone there, including me and James. Little Taffy looked the saddest of us all in her tiny black dress and bonnet.

Even so, some beams of joy managed to shine through the cold, dark clouds of grief. During Maximilian's lavish service we met Déjà, his lovely 20-year-old daughter whom we never knew he had. She is tall and brown haired like her father and shares his interest in motorcycles. Shortly after my husband and I met Déjà, we bonded with her and this family closeness further lifted the curse that had clutched the Schönhausses for so long.

What's more, even though the investigations that came in the aftermath of Maximilian's and Addy's apparent flaming demise had certainly been distressing for James, they also whetted his appetite to work for his expungement from the Silver City trailer park murder case. With that goal in mind, James pulled up stakes and moved with me and Taffy back to Silver City where we rented a house outside of town. Luckily, our landlord, a 75-year-old fellow named Gomez Piloncillo, loved monkeys. He had worked with more than one as a performer in a Tijuana-based circus during his youth.

In order to make ends meet, James and I went to work at the local Chinese restaurant, The Green Dragon, – he as a cook and me as one of the waitresses. Our landlord was only too happy to look after Taffy while we worked there. In his spare time, James eagerly pursued his goal of getting his felony conviction expunged. As a first step, he sent a written request to the New Mexico State Governor's Clemency Department. For the rest of the winter, the then Governor, Bill Richardson, reviewed James Schönhausse's manslaughter case, corresponded with him, and consulted with his staff on the issue. Finally, in early March, Gov. Richardson gained the best evidence of all in James' favor. A whole bundle of photos and e-mail printouts had somehow, mysteriously turned up in the ghost town of Curlew, North Dakota scathingly inditing certain members of the Silver City Police Department. James was even mentioned in a few of them as a fall guy. This slue of information revealed the real prison guard abuses which finally sparked the horrors of the New Mexico State Penitentiary riot and the massive cover up that went on for a decade afterward. The least of these excesses included guards routinely booting prisoners down long flights of stairs and subjecting them to tight overcrowding.

When my husband and I heard about Gov. Richardson receiving these eye opening documents and pictures from a contact who found them stashed in a Curlew storm cellar, we smiled and nodded our heads together.

"Bonnie love, how much do you want to bet that our friend Addy had a hand in this," said James cheerfully as he showed me his latest letter from Gov. Richardson.

"$9000 dollars to a donut," I replied with a wink. "He's an Angel. I'm sure of that now."

Indeed, he is. What's more, the papers that he made sure found their way into the New Mexico Governor's hands at the right moment were nothing short of Heaven sent. They did the trick for Bill Richardson. In a matter of days, he signed all of the right papers and James was given his long-hoped for expungement. Both of us were ecstatic and decided that a big celebration was in order. We put on a taco party or make shift fiesta and invited all of our friends and relatives to come and eat their fill of our homemade tacos.

"Tacos, tacos in the spring!" I sang as I served my guests while recalling the happiest train ride of my life.

Or was it only a dream? No matter.

Certainly, not everyone was happy with James' expungement and the spot light that flared on the New Mexico legal system as a result of it. In Silver City in particular the lid was ripped off a can of maggots that had been feeding on all levels of the police department for decades. As a result of the Governor's quick, decisive action, heads started to roll, in a manner of speaking. Especially that of the sly, duplicitous Detective Henry Hobbs who had worked so hard to frame James, but was now forced to retire from his position in disgrace. His ambition to be a judge would never be fulfilled.

With his name finally cleared of all bad connotations, life began to move swiftly and happily for James and our little family. We resigned from our jobs at the Green Dragon and he established his own newspaper, *The Silver City Daily*, which soon gained a huge readership and is now big competition for the City's original paper, the *Silver City Sun-News*. I meanwhile, focused on one of my major dream jobs – writing a book about New Mexico's wealth of breathtaking trees and flowers. The text of this colorful tome, which I gave the title of *Enchantment Blooms*, was embellished with my own illustrations and original poetry. Of course, James and I bought our house from Mr. Piloncillo and began to purchase several others for investment purposes.

I also returned to a craft that I had always enjoyed – the art of sewing. In my spare time I designed patterns and made clothes for men and women. These I sold on line and at a stand I would set up at Silver City's Art Market. Sometimes, James would help me run it. When it was his day for booth duty he would add his own handmade jewelry to the merchandise. When she wasn't busy with collage or dating, Déjà would volunteer to help too. No matter which of us humans would be there to tend the stall, Taffy would always be on hand. Inevitably she stole the show with her monkey antics and that helped move my crafts a lot quicker. Soon, I was adding my own line of cloth dolls and stuffed toy animals to the booth. These latter included, if you cared to class them as stuffed animals, a whimsical cloth creature called a "nauga".

A popular cloth toy in the 1970s, they were so-called because they were commonly made of naugahyde. Indeed, they were originally made by the company that first produced that fabric to promote its sale and use. The naugas themselves have the look of monsters that are more whimsical than scary with their jagged, fangy white cloth smile, squat bodies, and big round eyes. Their popularity had all but died off by the 2000s, so I decided to put my sewing skills to work and revive it. For this project, I bought a ton of naugahyde and got right to work. Soon, I had a horde of naugas of all sizes, from ones 3 inches tall to ones nearly 4 feet. I placed them in my booth and started selling them that same day. Soon, they were selling like Tootsie Pop Drops, another 70s top item. James and Déjà were both proud of me for fulfilling my dream of bringing the naugas back, so was Taffy in her own monkey way.

One morning after a day at the Art Market where I'd sold over a dozen naugas, I awoke to find one of my 12 inch nauga creations laying beside me on my pillow and James bending over me with a fond grin. He was holding Taffy who had a 4 inch one in her furry arms.

"How did you sleep after the big sale, sweet cheeks?" asked James who followed up his question with a kiss on my lips.

"Very well," I answered as I returned his kiss and gave Taffy a pat on the head. "And you, cute guy?"

"I never slept better in my life. I slept so well I had a dream. Want to hear about it?" asked James cheerfully.

"I sure do, Mr. Muscles. I tell you all my dreams and daydreams." I replied with a yawn as I slipped my bathrobe over my nightie.

"I dreamed I saw a hundred or more naugas lying in a field." he said as Taffy handed him the one she had been amusing herself with.

Being still half-asleep I misheard my husband say "nalgas", which is the Spanish word for "ass" or "posterior".

"I hope one of them was mine, cute guy," I replied with a hint of creeping jealousy.

"Ha ha. The cutest one was yours, sweet cheeks!" said James who had caught my misunderstanding and playfully slapped me on the rear. "But seriously I meant naugas, not nalgas.

"Oh," I said with a giggle, "pardon my thick head and stuffed ears this morning. By the way, I smell coffee."

"Come let's have some. Breakfast is nearly done." said James as I went with him to the kitchen where I would hold Taffy and enjoy my first morning cup of joe.

The naugas would continue to be my most popular item.

Another one of our favorite leisure time activities is urban archaeology. On one digging quest in particular we headed for the countryside on the edges of the city. I had awoke that bright morning of March 23, 2014 feeling a little tired and woozy and was still feeling that way as I rode along on Highway 180 headed for the proposed off-road site. Still, I wasn't going to let that hamper my day as I chatted lightly with James while balancing Taffy on my lap and admiring the trees and flowers crowning the sides of the road in abundance. Blooming desert willow, pretty in pink, was there in all its splendor towering over the white blossoms of yucca and the purple-blue carpets of periwinkle. To further sweeten this joyous spring scenario, a tiny rosy finch breezed by treating us to a snippet of song which was a rapid trill ending in a whistle.

Soon, we pulled over at the willow shaded turn-off where James was going to lead us on a hunt for history and, hopefully artifacts. An acquaintance of his in the city's Chamber of Commerce told him about this roadside spot where a cabin built in the late 1860s had once stood. James parked and all of us climbed out for a digging adventure. Even Taffy had a little pail and shovel. She and I followed James as he parted the fragrant branches for us. Just past the hedge of willows was a grassy bank decked with wildflowers and below that a seasonal creek gurgled merrily along. My sturdy husband removed a piece of paper from his overalls pocket and directed me and Taffy over to a spot under a pinion pine tree.

I looked at it closer and sure enough, there was the broken squarish frame of a very old house foundation. The crumbling granite rocks comprising it were so overgrown with moss that it was hard at first for me to distinguish it from the rest of the grass and moss covered forest floor. The closer I bent over it in order to make out its details, the damper and greener it smelled. I thought of a poem I had written once of a similar worn foundation I found while wondering the Canadian woods. This verse is titled "Old Stone Foundation" and reads as follows:

"Out in the field among the brambles,
Is an old house foundation where the weeds love to ramble,
Weathered gray stones form its broken sides and floor,
A hole gapes where there once were steps and a door,
Huge stone blocks which once were walls,
Crowd a partition which once was a hall,
To the side, a rusty stove, in the corner, a tree,
All over the cracked stones the moss and grass spread free,
Near every rounded corner grows a mullein plant so tall,
Like a yellow candlestick standing in a hall,
White pieces of porcelain lie strewn on the grass
With stones of every size and broken colored glass,
A few feet away is another stony place,
The moss-covered foundation of the home's outhouse space,
In my memory I will always hold fast,
This worn and weathered ghost of days long past."

And that also was a good description of the ruins I was looking over now. Its interior was just waiting for us to explore it.

"This is where we start digging, girls," said James as he pushed his own shovel into the center of the broken foundation with clinical precision.

A moment later he lifted out a clump of black hummus laced with long pale green roots and alive with wriggling earthworms. On that cue, me and Taffy started digging too. In a short time, we had dug down 3 feet or more and were already unearthing objects of interest. Once we got past the initial layers of soil and rocks we began to find items that were part of the household that once stood proudly on the moss choked foundation. James and I unearthed a couple of intact china plates, some real silverware, a silver candle stick, some rusty remains of tin cans, a clock, a few clock parts, various glass bottles, and a monocle. Even Taffy found something – a wooden top that still worked even though the paint on it had long worn off.

At that point, I was starting to feel really tired and was about to insist that we give up our digging for the day and count our finds. Then I noticed an interesting bulge in the soil. Exploring it with my fingers I pulled out a 3-inch china baby doll as though birthing it from the womb of Mother Earth.

"Why, Bonnie love, you found a 3-month-old fetus!" exclaimed James with teasing interest.

"Yes, I have, cute guy, and in more ways than one," I said, implying that my tiredness and the queasiness I felt earlier were not the result of me having a "bug."

"Bonnie, you're going to have my child! I'm going to be a dad!" he replied, beside himself with bursting joy.

"Yes, indeed I am, Mr. Muscles!" I said with a giggle as I wiped more dirt from my porcelain "baby" and held it up proudly.

The tiny doll was without a mar or chip and in the muted light, looked like the real thing.

For a list of all available books by
Everlasting Publishing, please visit our website:
everlastingpublishing.org